Secrets and Wishes

Also by Liz Newton and published by Ginninderra Press
The Firing Line

Liz Newton

Secrets and Wishes

Acknowledgements

I wish to thank those friends and family members who have reviewed
these stories and offered insight along the way.
Over many years, the Common Thread writing group has provided
support, critical appraisal and encouragement.
Thank you to my publisher Ginninderra Press
for bringing the manuscript to reality.

For my family

Secrets and Wishes
ISBN 978 1 76109 364 7
Copyright © text Liz Newton 2022

First published 2022 by
GINNINDERRA PRESS
PO Box 3461 Port Adelaide 5015
www.ginninderrapress.com.au

Contents

Secrets and Wishes

I'm inside the shed and I can't tell if it's day or night. The metal shipping container, which had been turned into Dad's shed, sat on the dirt across the creek from our house. I am now five years old, but it's still a scary place. The small, barred window at the far end of the container was sunny one minute and now dark. Even I know the sun doesn't go down so quickly. The sun then peeped back again, filling the empty space with light. I remember Mum saying, 'Isabella, there's going to be an eclipse soon.' She explained it was when the sun hides for a while just to scare people, before it pops back to let us know how wonderful the universe really is. Now I know it's Sunday because that's when the eclipse was going to happen.

It was light outside once more, yet I was shivering, even though I'd stretched my pink jumper over my knees when I sat.

I can't unsee the things I saw earlier this morning. I tried to block them out by wiping my eyes over and over. It didn't work. I can't unhear the screeches I'd heard.

In the distance, the fading sirens were now a dull hum.

A churning tummy made vomit rise in my throat, so I sucked in my cheeks, which tasted like a rusty pipe. My tongue felt the hole where blood seeped from a new toothless cave in my mouth.

The old shed smelled of oil and hay. I could see the dilapidated tractor in the corner. Strewn on the ground were tools which couldn't fix it. The feed tray attached at the rear was empty.

How long had I been asleep? Was it hours, or more than a day?

The last touch, the one I'll never forget, was when Mum's warm hand stroked my face. 'Shush, won't be long now, don't say a word. It's our secret,' she said.

I nodded to let Mum know that now I was five, I knew about secrets and how to make wishes. I'd started big school a few weeks ago and the girls played a game of whispering: I've got a secret and I won't tell. So I knew to keep quiet, otherwise things wouldn't come true.

Mum walked away, slammed the container door shut and bolted it with a lock. The keys jangled for a few seconds, before I heard them plop outside into the nearby water trough.

I closed my eyes, humming a silent lullaby in my head, while willing for Mum to come back.

Sometime later, I awoke again to find a plastic bag left near the doorway. Inside was a sooty-smelling blanket, a large water bottle, some fruit and chips, and my second-best teddy, the brown one. Why didn't anyone in my whole family remember I have a list from one to three, for my Brownie teddy, Fluffy bear and the purple one with the ribbon? The best teddy for the week, which should have been Fluffy bear, gets to sleep on my pillow. I felt tears leaking and buried my face under the blanket, wondering where Fluffy was now.

I nodded off when the sun was going down and the light fading. A loud crack of thunder woke me. Then I heard splats of rain on the tin roof, which soon became louder when the rain pelted hard, so I tried to cover my ears, but it didn't help much. I was worried now, so I tucked Brownie under the rug and sang a song – even though no one would hear me singing with the racket outside. I told Brownie the story of how my little brother Robbie wandered away towardss the river and slipped on the muddy bank, just when Dad arrived to scoop him up. Dad said he followed Robbie's little footprints to find him. Eventually, Brownie and I both went to sleep, happy to know someone always saves little kids, and even the creepiest stories have happy endings.

The rain had stopped by morning and a few last drips were forming little rivers down the steel wall, leaving a couple of puddles in a low-lying corner of the floor. I wanted to play and splash with Brownie, ex-cept I slipped, and my bear fell face down, now soaking wet. Brownie looked as sad as I felt because I knew whenever there was lots of rain near our house it washed away all the tyre prints and tracks. I also remembered that after enormous storms, the river swelled so much even Dad's ute couldn't get across the creek for days. That meant he couldn't reach the shed where the broken farm equipment was dumped. So how would anyone find us here now?

My next day in the container was Monday. I wanted to make it a day of discovery for Brownie and me. I had to make up games to cheer him up, so I started with 'I spy'. There wasn't a lot to see but it helped the time go faster. The broken-down tractor was great for climbing on, so I pretended to shift the gears and steer the wheel, while I took Brownie on a drive around our paddocks.

'See that, Brownie? Look at how green the grass is. The cows are chomping away on every bit. Now they're so full they need to lie in the shade of the big tree. And look in the distance, Brownie. It's our house. We'll be home soon and you can sleep in my bed – in fact, for a special treat, all three of you bears can sleep with me.'

I started to cry, wondering what had just happened at home. I wasn't sure why Mum bundled Robbie and me in the car and buckled us up before she raced back inside for something – she was always forgetting things. But I did remember her saying I had to stay put in the shed, while she took Robbie somewhere, because I talked too much.

I climbed down from the tractor and showed Brownie around the container to take my mind away from scary things. Brownie and I found all sorts of broken tools and bits and pieces of rusted metal. There was an old chair and three cardboard boxes taped up with the silver duck stuff, the tape that's hard to undo.

I grabbed a rusty screwdriver and ripped at the edges to open the boxes. One was full of old paper with lots of numbers in rows down the page, and some letters. I could read some words but not these ones, and knew nearly all my numbers, but these looked like millions. I could only count to a hundred.

'Nothing interesting here, Brownie. Let's have some lunch and then we'll explore the next box.'

I sat in the lounge chair, which was torn at the edges. It was much more comfortable than the cold floor. There was room for Brownie to snuggle beside me while I rummaged through the plastic bag for food. There were three small bags of chips, two apples, half a packet of arrowroot biscuits and a full packet of seaweed rice crackers. At least Mum knew they were my favourites. Brownie shared the food and I ate the broken biscuits because Brownie couldn't swallow them. After a drink of water, I wiped his face and we decided to open another box.

'Now sit, Brownie, and don't go away, while I get this duck tape off.' Funny stuff, I thought, and I suddenly remembered what Dad said. 'Not duck, Izzy, *duct*.' At the time, I laughed and wondered what it had to do with ducks. I still don't understand why it's called that.

After lots of stabbing and ripping, the box was open. I scrabbled through, lifting out lots of fading colour photos and little books, which had writing only and no pictures, along with a few old keys on a silver ring. At the bottom lay a framed large photo with Dad and a very young girl with her arms cuddling a boy about my age. It must be Mum, I thought, so I looked closer. Yes, it was her, same green eyes, and curly hair, like me. The boy also had green eyes and curly hair. If he weren't a boy, he would look almost like me. The photo was faded, but Dad still looked the same, because he'd always had a beard and brushed his hair back.

'Where are you now, Dad?' I shouted into the container and heard a faint echo bounce back.

I stared at the boy's photo again, wondering who he was. Mum seemed to like him. She was smiling and hugging him. I thought of my little brother Robert. I really missed him, even though he was a pest when he messed up my drawings and wanted to play with my stuff all the time. Mum always said, 'Look after Robbie, I'm busy.' All she did was stare into space and talk on the phone.

On the back of the photo, a couple of words were written, which I could read. It said, 'John 4 years, Maggie and Matt 2012'. I had a friend at school called John, so I knew the word. I also could read Mum and Dad's names because I'd read them on cards and notes.

Then I found some more pictures. There was one of Mum and me as a baby, which said, 'Isabella 2018'. I uncovered more photos of me as a little girl with my teddies, but not one of me as a big five-year-old. There were a couple of Robbie with me and Mum and Dad, and one with Gran and Grandpa, but no more of the boy called John.

The afternoon was long and the shadows coming from the sun shining from the high window gradually disappeared. Brownie had been playing hide and seek with me and I did some running up and down the container to see if I could beat him – but I had to carry him and pretend he won sometimes. The games made us hungry, so I got our dinner ready and set the food out on an upturned box. We ate another apple and nearly all the rice crackers before it got dark.

I tried to do normal things and made Brownie do them also. We washed our faces and smoothed our hair – Mum didn't leave a toothbrush or soap, so we had to make do and used water from the puddles. Dad was the one who usually told me to scrub my teeth and brush my hair, yet it still seemed to tangle in the slightest wind. Going to the toilet was a bit harder to work out but Brownie didn't really need to go, so I found a small gaping slit on one of the side floors and did my wee there. Eventually, I would need to do number two – so Mum better be back by then.

Night time was coming again and usually I went to sleep with a story from my mum or dad and cuddles from my little brother. I didn't have a night light here, which made everything seemed bigger and scary. I was frightened and worried, wondering when Mum or Dad would ever come. I didn't want Brownie getting upset, so I sang songs and told him a few stories I'd learnt from school. He yawned and so did I. Time to sleep.

*

Matt Rushmore parked his truck metres from the unloading yard. Dust flew up from the brakes, temporarily obscuring his vision and wafting towardss the snorting cattle. He'd been on the road with his cattle-dog mate Bluey from sunup, on what began like any other Sunday, hauling the cattle four hours to a neighbouring big town ready for the sales on Monday. Matt had no sooner arrived with his load than a police officer pulled him aside and relayed the news of what had happened to his house.

Matt immediately got stuck into his work of unloading the cattle from the rear of the truck with Bluey, who loved the job of barking and circling them into the holding yard. Matt then filled the tank at the local servo, grabbed a takeaway sandwich and coffee, and hit the tarmac once more. Trying not to break the speed limit, he set the truck's cruise control a tad high, enough to gain a little time and hopefully not cop a fine and demerit points. *What the hell has Maggie done now, and where are the kids?* The police hadn't expanded any further. The only news he'd received was to get home fast and talk to the local command cops, who were waiting to fill him in.

Less than two hours later, the first drops of rain muddied the dust on the windscreen and minutes later it bucketed down for the remainder of the journey.

'Nearly there, Blue,' he said, rounding the final bend through the front gate of his property.

He couldn't believe what he wasn't seeing. There was no house. The fire engine sat with lights flashing and hoses unreeled while half a dozen firefighters combed the wreckage. A single police car was parked in front of the fire zone, which was now smouldering into a blackened muddy mess from the recent heavy rain.

Matt screeched the truck to a halt and ran towardss the skeleton of charred timbers. 'Where are they? What the fuck happened?'

'Can't say for sure, Matt, but come away from there, the structure's not stable,' the constable said.

'What about my kids?'

'It doesn't look like they were home. There was no car here and we tried to ring your wife's mobile, but it went straight to voicemail. The fire fighters think an upturned radiator may have started the blaze.

Don't know for sure. May have been something else. Do you know where your wife might have gone?'

'Not sure, maybe her mother's place, about an hour away. She never tells me where she goes. I'll try the in-laws on their landline.' Matt stared to scroll through his mobile contacts when he heard a shout.

'Over here,' one of the firemen yelled.

Constable Baker ran to the scene, with Matt one step behind.

'Looks like bones of a child, maybe four or five years old.'

Matt's knees buckled and he collapsed into the mud. 'Noooo…' he cried.

Constable Baker briefly examined the findings and looked to Matt. 'We'll need to have tests done by the coroner, and possibly a DNA match. There's nothing more you can do here, Matt. However, given the circumstances, you'd better come down to the station with me.'

Bewildered, Matt shook his head. 'What for? Do you think I did it? I left at sparrow's fart this morning. Maggie, Rob and Izzy were sound asleep. I'm not going anywhere until I've found my family.'

'Matt, you can't stay here, and the creek's flooded. Now, you either come down to the station quietly or I'll arrest you.'

'Okay, okay. No drama. I'll come and you do whatever you need to do. THEN I'm going to look for my kids.'

*

It was a long and frustrating evening for Matt as he paced the cell and underwent questioning and DNA sampling. He was told it would take a while to see if his sample matched the mitochondrial DNA of the child's bones found at his house. He begged to use his mobile phone after the police had checked and recorded the recent numbers called. Eventually, the phone was returned to Matt who, while waiting for interviews and the paperwork to be completed, rang his wife's number constantly. However, it went to voicemail each time.

Matt then tried his in-laws, who said they hadn't seen Maggie since they were over for dinner with the kids the previous weekend. He explained the situation to his father-in-law while he heard his ageing mother-in-law wail in the background. 'What has she done now, those poor little kiddies?'

The police constable returned to tell Matt he was now free to go, though he warned him not to leave the local area in case he was required for further questioning. It was late and the evening sky darkened. Matt had nowhere to stay, yet he was damned sure he wasn't going to waste time hanging around the police station. He was convinced no one was doing anything to try and find his kids. Outside the door, Matt headed for the servo, grabbed two burgers, one each for himself and Bluey. He plugged his now dead mobile into the car socket to recharge and began talking to his dog. 'Where is she? What next? Where should we look?'

Exhausted, Matt rolled up his coat for a pillow and lay across the bench seat of his truck, with Bluey at his feet, hoping to grab a few hours' sleep before dawn – when his mind cleared, he'd work out a plan.

Bluey was the first to squirm when the sun rose. He nudged his master to open the door so he could pee. The rain had dwindled to a light drizzle and luckily the servo opened early. After a quick wash, and a couple of egg and bacon sandwiches, they set off.

Arriving at the charred site of his home, Matt noticed it was still cordoned off as a crime scene, because of the child's bones they'd found. How on earth did the bones get there, he asked himself.

He and Maggie had relocated to the property from another outback town interstate about six years ago before Izzy was born. He thought Maggie had left her anguish behind when she found out she was pregnant again.

Matt fiddled around the edges of the burnt-out house trying to salvage anything he considered still useful, or which might have some importance to him and his family. Nevertheless, there wasn't much worth saving. No kid's toys, no jewellery, no clothes, and the crockery they were given for a wedding present was all broken.

'Come on, Bluey, let's go and find them.' Matt whistled and Bluey jumped in the back of the ute.

The creek water was still up. It would be late in the day, Matt reckoned, before it receded enough for him to cross. Matt was certain the evidence from the bones was definitely going to be a match, and without photos of the boy they once had, or evidence Izzy was still alive, he would have a lot of convincing to do with the police, to clear himself. He decided his first task was to cross the creek when it eventually subsided, and retrieve the photos of their first-born John, in case the police came snooping around the rest of his property.

Meanwhile, Matt headed towardss his in-laws' house to try and get some sense out of his mother in-law, knowing Maggie phoned her regularly and had probably been in touch by now. Maggie's parents greeted him at the door, desperate to hear any news of their daughter and the kids. Cec, his father-in-law, stoic as usual, tried to calm and settle his wife.

Matt's mother-in-law, Dot, began wailing again. 'She shouldn't have been let out of the hospital after Johnnie died. I know it was an accident, but sometimes she made wild claims. I can't remember her even crying at the little mite's funeral. Everyone said she was in shock. But I knew better. Maggie's been like it since a kid, only ever interested in herself and what she could get from others.' Dot shook her head in disbelief. 'She's still my daughter and I love her, and those beautiful grandkids.'

'Enough, Dot. Matt's here to try and find out where she might be.'

Matt sat quietly, knowing if they had any clues, his in-laws would be forthcoming. Until now, though, they had nothing to add. The pain of watching them despair grated on his nerves. He didn't dare broach the subject of little John's grave, which he knew Maggie had organised to be dug up by a local drug-addicted guy for five hundred dollars. She had a fixed idea in her head she should keep the tiny skeleton. In fact, Matt wasn't sure if his in-laws even knew about it, though Maggie did say at the time they gave her money towardss a headstone. Best not mention it, he decided. Matt and Maggie's child's death had been the impetus for moving townships at the time, an attempt to avoid any gossip or suspicion.

Matt rested for a while longer, drank two more cups of tea, then feigned tiredness and the need to get back to his property in case of looting. He also knew the local coppers would soon match the DNA samples from the boxes to himself. The police still believed it was his daughter's bones which were in his burnt-out house. He needed to find his family – fast.

It had been a long day and dusk was closing in. Thankfully, the creek was now low enough for Matt to drive the truck through when he'd returned from the in-laws. He noticed some tyre tracks in the muddy ground. Bloody cops, he immediately thought, or maybe just a neighbouring farmer. No need for alarm, he told himself.

When he reached the container, Matt found the lock undone and the boxes of photos and books in the corner. He used his phone torch to search around, which illuminated an empty chip packet, fresh apple cores, and a single hair clip – the mauve plastic bow which Izzy used for her purple teddy. Apart from those things, the container was pretty much empty, and left as he'd last seen it, with the old chair and tools scattered and the boxes of books and photos. The boxes had been opened, yet only two of the three were left in the shed. Matt didn't know what to make of it, though the churn in his gut told him Maggie was somehow involved.

*

Maggie Rushmore squirmed in the front seat of her Holden station wagon when she leant over to keep her two children quiet with another lollipop.

'I don't want one, Mummy,' Izzy said. 'I just want to go home. It's getting dark.'

'We need to wait under these trees, so no one sees us until the creek is down a bit more.'

'But I'm scared, and Brownie is too.' Izzy began flicking all the internal light buttons on and off in the car, including leaning over to flick the switches in the rear of the wagon.

'Stop that!' Maggie slapped her legs. 'Turn them off.'

'Which ones? I can't find all the buttons in the dark.'

'Shit! You stupid girl, one day you'll go where Johnnie went.'

Izzy started to cry while Maggie cuddled Robbie, who was content with the extra lollipop.

'See, Izzy, Robbie's being a good boy. Do you want to spend another night locked in the container?'

Maggie watched Izzy cower in the fading light. She knew her daughter would be imagining her father looking for tracks to find her, which he'd done in the past, but this time the rain had washed them away.

What Maggie didn't know was, when Izzy flicked the internal car lights on, she had alerted Matt from afar.

*

Matt had enough sense to stay still and make a plan before his wife sped off, which he knew she'd do when she thought the creek was down enough for her low-bodied car to cross. He watched and waited for any sign of movement. The best course of action, he determined, was to push his ute out of gear, towardss the creek, and sit tight until they attempted to cross. Matt also realised he'd have to be ready to swerve in front of Maggie's car before she reached the dip in the watercourse.

When the sun dipped below the horizon, Matt heard the motor of the station wagon and seconds later, dappled headlights shone through the trees. Matt knew his wife's driving style well, and while she was a bit of a lead-foot on a straight road, she always slowed down at the creek. Too easy, he thought, when the wagon almost reached the dip. He flicked on his headlights and crossed in front, bringing both vehicles to a halt.

Maggie jumped out of the car and screeched at her husband. 'What the hell do you think you're doing?'

'Getting my kids back now – safe and alive.'

'No way!' Maggie clicked the central locking on the wagon and flung the keys in the creek. She picked up a rock and tossed it overarm, barely missing Matt's head when he ducked.

Bluey growled and barked incessantly, spinning in circles, snapping close to Maggie's feet. Matt grabbed his wife before she could do more harm or attempt to flee.

A squeal of sirens spun across the muddy plain and careered to a stop skidding in the dirt.

Constable Baker bolted out. 'Thought I'd find you here, Matt. Seems like we found more than we bargained for. What's going on? And call your bloody dog off!'

'It's not me. Ask her what happened.' Tears welled in Matt's eyes when he reluctantly spoke about his wife's behaviour, the woman he loved, and had tried to protect at any cost. He looked squarely at Maggie. 'I'm not going down for what you've done.'

Izzy banged loudly on the car window.

'Maggie's thrown the keys in the creek. Is there any way you can break the locks?' Matt asked.

The constable instantly tilted his head towardss the racket coming from the station wagon.

Once the children were freed, Constable Baker looked quizzically at Matt. 'Your two kids are safe, so whose bones were they?'

'It's a long story and I need to be with my kids right now,' Matt urged, and he gathered them tight in his arms.

Constable Baker nodded and left him with Izzy and Robbie, who were crying, unable to comprehend the situation they were in, especially seeing their mum sobbing in the back of a police car.

'It'll be okay. We'll go and stay at Grandma's for a while until things settle down.'

'You found us, Daddy, you followed the tracks, even when Mummy said they were all washed away.'

'They were all washed away, sweetie, but I noticed flickering lights through the bushes. I thought there was a car in the distance, so I crept closer to investigate.'

'I punched the light buttons,' Izzy beamed.

'I thought it was you. Good thinking. But do you know what the biggest problem was?'

The children, along with Brownie bear, shook their heads.

'It was Bluey. He must have sensed something, and he was itching to go and find you. I had to lock him in the car so he didn't give me away.'

They all giggled while Bluey yapped with delight chasing his own tail.

Constable Baker broke up the reunion. 'Matt, can you get anyone to mind the kids? I need you down at the station with your wife. It could take some time.'

'Sure. I'll get the in-laws to pick them up for the night.'

*

The station buzzed with reporters milling outside wondering what the story was, and impatiently waiting to have the first police report to slam over the front pages the following morning. However, it took some time for the police to fill in the gaps and piece together what had occurred.

Maggie was the first to be interviewed, while Matt was arranging for the children to be looked after. By the time it was his turn to sit in the interview room, his wife was wailing incoherently. A specialist mental health assessment was called for. His heart ached when she was taken away to be sedated, before being transferred to the nearest contained facility.

Nevertheless, Matt was determined not to let her get away with murder again, especially after Izzy told him her mum threatened to send her to be with Johnnie. Matt was convinced Maggie needed expert care and at least she would get it now. He craved that no more damage could come to his family. Matt felt guilty at having protected her for so long and wondered if his kids would ever get over the trauma. He prayed that, with help, he could undo some of their bad memories and refashion them into something else. It was going to be his long-term plan, but for now Matt needed to come clean with Constable Baker.

The story Matt told was of an attractive young girl in her late teens who he'd met at the local rodeo. Maggie loved horses and rode well.

They had a lot in common and Matt was thrilled when she accepted his marriage proposal. Maggie seemed constantly bubbly and happy, and while Matt sometimes thought she was a bit over the top, he accepted her being the life of any party. Until she found out she was pregnant. Maggie seemed to slump into negativity and worried constantly until John was born. Her parents were a great comfort, to both him and Maggie during the pregnancy, and after their first baby was born. However, Maggie seemed to grow more anxious and muddled. She was eventually put under the care of the health service and a counsellor who visited infrequently, though in their town, they were fortunate to have a city psychiatrist visit monthly, who reviewed her situation and medications.

Time went on, with many mishaps during John's early years growing up. Often, he had bruises, which Maggie explained were from falling over or climbing. On a couple of occasions when Matt returned from long days rounding up cattle, he'd find Maggie asleep and John playing with matches or knives.

The final incident occurred when Johnnie and his mum went for a play in the shallows of their dam. Maggie screamed for help, running to the shed where Matt was fixing the trailer. Apparently, their little boy had slipped on the muddy bank and into the deep water. Johnnie was unable to swim to shore. Instead of assisting him, Maggie had run nearly ten minutes back to their homestead and by the time Matt raced back to the dam, John was dead.

Matt recalled how Maggie had looked puzzled when he told her she should have attempted to save her son. He was shocked when his wife replied softly, 'I did what I had to do, Matt.'

Tears ran down Matt's sunbaked face as he related the story to Constable Baker and then he told of more recent incidents when Izzy, then Robbie, were born. With his help, Maggie seemed to manage when they were little but when John and Izzy became more independent, Maggie found it increasingly difficult to cope. She had a few hospitalisations in the ensuing years and was discharged on psychiatric medications, which she took haphazardly, and she lied to Matt about what she was, or was not, taking.

Matt put his head in his hands. His shoulders slumped. 'I never should have left Maggie with them, never should have trusted her after Johnnie. I thought by leaving the last outback town, we could start afresh. My only wish was for us to be happy. It was okay for a while but lately Maggie seemed to be derailing again.' He sighed and then added, 'Izzy told me earlier today that before her mother took her to the container, Maggie had locked them in the car and told her not to tell anyone about their trip. Izzy watched her Mum do something at the side of the car, before racing back into the house with a wet smelly rag. When I asked her about the rag, she said it smelled like the pump at the servo.'

Constable Baker spoke. 'Matt, she's in care now and you did whatever you could. I've no doubt you saved those two kids today. I want you to go out the back door with one of my officers and be with your kids. I now need to make a statement for the feeding frenzy outside.'

The Piano

Each day lingered until darkness merged into a fitful night, yet still Joe could not bring himself to make the journey. Nagging thoughts sparked within him, only to be blocked to the far recess of his mind. Nevertheless, he would compel himself to head to Sydney soon. He dreaded watching the hustle and bustle of ant-sized people darting between honking traffic, lost in the shadows of tall buildings. If the truth be known, it scared him.

Joe had farmed the land for all his adult life. The early days were fruitful, enabling Joe's family, his wife and two daughters, to holiday over at the coast each summer. More recently, though, each year became harsher. The drought set in. It was relentless watching the parched earth crack open like a gash without a drop of blood. Life on the land seemed to worsen daily and any profits diminished to nothing. Joe ceased caring. The future was bleak. He felt his heart harden, but it wouldn't stop beating. He despaired, unable to fathom a way out.

Joe's girls eventually grew up. His youngest had left the farm to travel to the city, while his eldest now worked in a regional town. There was certainly nothing left out west any more to entice the next generation to stay.

Joe pondered how his grandfather, when a young man with a growing family, had survived the Depression in the 1930s. It was not long after the First World War ended, when people looked triumphantly for a brighter future. Then crash, the hard times hit with a vengeance, soon to be followed by another war. Growing up, Joe relished his grandfather's stories. He especially liked the ones of his Nan making do with whatever food they had, kneading a flour damper to lash with dripping. That would sustain their hungry kids, along with transient men searching for work.

He also liked his grandfather's story of creative ways to feed his family, when at the peak of the Depression, he'd resorted to pinching fruit and fresh vegetables off the newly filled-in graves of dead Chinamen at the Gore Hill Cemetery, in Sydney. The burial ground was not far from where his grandparents lived at the time in Artarmon. Joe heard the stories of Chinese people's innovative ways to keep up their food supply. He learnt they were skilful gardeners and could manage to grow anything in their backyards, turning them into market gardens. Joe's grandad said it was no use leaving the food there rotting when his kids were starving at home.

Back to his present dilemma, Joe focused once more on his own family and their future. He'd let them down; he was a failure – defeated. The bank was foreclosing on his mortgage, probably a good thing, he reasoned, because the drought had no end in sight. His kids had moved out and his wife, he believed, would be better off with the insurance payout if he died. It was his only answer, to put an end to this mess.

Nonetheless, Joe was adamant he'd set things straight before he died. He would settle whatever debts he could. He certainly wasn't going to leave this earth without paying back the Chinese people who fed his ancestors all those years ago. It meant he could leave this world in peace, and at this point, peace was all he craved. He ached to be free from the dread which gnawed his gut every day – and broke his heart.

Eventually, the day came when Joe woke with a vexing sense of urgency. When up and dressed for the day, he slung his bag over his shoulder and kissed his wife goodbye. She didn't suspect anything unusual when her husband announced he was going into town to get the paper, maybe check out the price of cattle and perhaps have a yarn with a few locals. Joe filled his knapsack with packet crackers and as many loose coins he could forage from the spare change biscuit tin. He intended to buy mandarins, bananas, fresh tomatoes and whatever else he imagined his granddad might have stolen off the graves. Joe wanted to exit with a clear conscience and a clean slate. Silly idea, he thought to himself. As if anyone might notice or care.

Joe alighted from the country train platform at Central Station. Lugging his laden bag, he headed off. Up the escalator he strode two steps at a time, until his energy depleted. The metal escalator teeth seemed to be mocking him as he ascended. In his mind, they distorted into jaws of death. His hands sweated and he gasped for breath, anxious to reach the top. Once he hit the daylight, he jostled to change trains onto the northern line bound for St Leonards.

It was a short walk to the cemetery. Through the rusty metal gates, Joe wandered aimlessly among eroded sandstone crosses and memorials, many from the 1800s. Spiky tufts of grass surrounded the graves and buttercup yellow wildflowers popped up sporadically. The words and dates on the memorials were faded and chipped. The cemetery was bigger than he imagined, sprawling over a couple of blocks. Joe stopped to ask a gardener where the Chinese section from the early 1900s was located. After being pointed in the right direction, he finally found some overgrown smaller stones with age-worn Chinese characters. It seemed as if no one had been this way for some time. He placed fruit in small piles on the graves, closed his eyes and thanked them for providing food all those years ago. Quietly he bowed his head and prayed to his grandad. 'I'll see you soon.'

Satisfied with making amends Joe was ready to complete his journey. He mapped out in his mind his next steps. Firstly, he'd take the train back to city, then later catch the ferry to Watson's Bay, before a long stroll up the grassy slope to the Gap. With a single step over the cliff's edge, he'd be gone. At least he'd be able to feel the wind and salt-spray on his dry skin when he fell. In the end, he would welcome being immersed in the ocean – anything was better than the incessant inland dust.

When Joe reached Wynyard Station, the sunshine radiated a little warmth on his cheeks, light as a feather, unlike the harsh scorching days at the farm. He dawdled towards Hyde Park to loiter a while and make calls to his wife and daughters – just to say goodbye, to hear their voices one last time, before he went to the Quay to catch the ferry to Watson's Bay. Three goodbyes. Who to ring first, he pondered?

Resting on a bench under a strangler fig, Joe heard a tinkling piano melody. Maybe it was from a concert at the Conservatorium. How could he hear it from over there? Must be going mad, he thought. Standing, he shook his head to clear his suffocating mind. The music lured him along before he stopped and noticed a girl, a young woman, sitting at a grand piano. Her flaxen hair cascaded down her back, while her fingers danced across the piano keys to the tune of *Fur Elise*. To Joe, it seemed like yesterday when he was a kid taking piano lessons.

The girl was playing the tune very well, though, which was evident from her busking bucket filling with coins and notes. It reminded Joe of his days at the Tamworth Music Festival when a young lad. Things are pretty fancy down here, though, he mused. How on earth did the piano get in the park? Strange things happen in big cities. Joe smiled, which gave him a jolt. It had been a long time since he'd felt his veins fizz and eyes crinkle. A trickle of hope seeped from his heart. Joe edged to the front of the piano, hesitated, and tilted his head.

The face of his daughter glowed back at him. 'What are you doing here, Dad?'

Mouth agape, Joe stared. It really was his beloved youngest daughter.

'Dad?'

'I... I...just wanted to say g...g...'

'What, Dad?'

'...to say hello.'

'Well, hi to you too, Dad. Come and join me. Play the chords.'

Locked Away

It was the late 1970s and Christmas was fast approaching. Rosa smiled at her wide-eyed three-year-old twin boys while she stirred soaked fruit into the dry pudding ingredients. Lifting the mixing bowl, she expertly scooped the lot into the steamer pot and secured the lid tight, now ready to boil for a couple of hours. The boys squabbled like two young joeys over who would scrape the bowl or lick the spoon.

Their father walked into the kitchen and separated them. 'Smells great. Best thing about Christmas is Mum's plum pudding, eh, boys.'

The boys nodded, savouring every last lick of pudding batter from their sticky fingers.

Rosa loved the chaos of Christmas Day. Presents and wrapping everywhere, squeals of delight and mountains of home-cooked goodies. She had prepared weeks beforehand for a perfect day. However, she lamented the one thing which was missing.

Rosa, pleased to see her husband Marco in one of his rare cheerful moods, chatted away about the vegie garden and asked how the hens were laying before attempting to change the subject. 'Do you think we could bring Linny home for Christmas Day this year?' she pleaded.

Rosa's attempt to segue the conversation fell into nothingness. Silence.

Marco shook his head and trudged back outdoors to his chores. It was the same response he'd given over the last few years.

Rosa dabbed an escaping tear with the tea towel and whispered, 'My darling Linny.'

Rosa was fully aware Marco's nerves were frayed at the possibility of another of Linny's uncontrollable shrieking and spitting fits. Those times usually ended with Linny pecking at her food before flinging it around the room. Sadly, Linny seemed completely unable to understand or respond to simple commands. In the early days, Marco had tried in his own way to make his daughter understand enough to do as she was told. He even took her outside for long periods into their market garden and poultry farm on the outskirts of Sydney. However, all Linny seemed to want to do was scratch in the dirt and roll on the grass for hours on end. It was his way of giving Rosa a break to clean up Linny's smeared food and other messes inside the house. Yet nothing seemed to alter her behaviour. In the end, Marco became rattled and jittery at the mere sight of Linny. His annoyance was quick to unravel into a rage whenever attempting to put limits around her actions, shrieks and squeals.

Rosa's heart broke one night when she watched her then four-year-old Linny bolt to her bedroom like a beaten whippet racing to its kennel. It was soon after the episode when Rosa, seven months pregnant, attended a joint consultation with their local doctor and a social worker. They agreed it was best for their daughter to be placed in an institution. It was explained to the parents the asylum was a place of refuge, where Linny would be cared for day and night. Once Rosa's boys were born, Marco progressively shied away from any conversation about Linny. Unlike her husband, who seemed relieved his daughter was gone, Rosa was determined never to forget her golden-haired girl.

Linny, now aged eight, had resided in the island institution on the Hawkesbury River since the mid-1970s. At the end of the next week, as she had done many times in the last few years, Rosa would make the trek by bus and train early on Christmas morning to spend time with her daughter. It would be the usual long day for Rosa, while Marco and the boys awaited her return to serve an evening family Christmas dinner.

*

Arriving for a morning shift on the island, Mandy yawned and plonked herself on the orange vinyl chair in the ward office.

'You're late again, Mandy.'

'Sorry, Rick. These early starts kill me.' She yawned again and abruptly closed her mouth when Rick shot her a displeasing look.

He then pointed towards the overflowing cardboard box in the corner. 'We've got a lot to do today, Mandy, and you can help me hang a few more of those Christmas decorations.'

'Not bloody Christmas again. Why do we bother?' Mandy sighed. 'These kids couldn't care less. It's just one more day of screeching and fighting. And a big mess to clean up.'

Rick took in a deep breath and wondered at his workmate's lack of compassion towards the forgotten children on the island. 'Hey, why don't you just pretend you're enjoying it and the work won't be so bad. They need a break in routine and whatever you think, these little things DO make a difference for the kids.'

'Kids! Ha! More like animals if you ask me.' Reluctantly, Mandy pulled herself off the chair, swigged a last mouthful of coffee and stubbed out her cigarette. 'Okay, let's do it. After we've got them up and hosed down – sorry, I mean showered – we'll let them loose on the box of tinsel.'

The Christmas tree stood bare in the corner of the linoleum floor in the lounge. Rick walked over with a bundle of decorations, some ageing with bits missing and others made by the kids, including a couple of lengths of paper chain glued together by the older children. Reaching deep into another cupboard, Rick pulled out a dozen silver paper lanterns, homemade by him when last on night duty. The paper slits were neater than when he'd made similar ones in his childhood and they still brought him joy to see the lanterns hung.

When Mandy slunk off to get the girls up and dressed, Rick called after her. 'By the way, I'm working on Christmas Day with you this year, so let's make it a fun day.'

'Don't bloody remind me. I wish I was home with my own family but I got rostered on so the staff with their own kids could have the day off.'

'It's fair enough, don't you think? It means we get New Year's Eve off. It's always worked that way.'

Christmas Day rapidly eventuated and the institution staff held small parties in each ward, as much to amuse themselves and break the monotony as to give the children something special to look forward to. Many of the youngsters sat sullen in the corners of the large airy rooms, while others seemed to revel in any change of activity.

Ben, who was nearly eleven, always endeavoured to get involved. He often spent time hanging around the staff when some of the littlies had gone to bed. Ben knew if he wasn't a bother, then perhaps whoever was working the evening shift would let him watch a bit more television, including his favourite show, *The Flintstones*.

Each day, the routine began at dawn when the children woke. Some wailed and squirmed until they'd been cleaned and dressed for breakfast, while others never muttered a sound. Large white cotton bibs were fastened around the kids' necks, before staff shovelled sloppy food into those who couldn't manage to hold a spoon or a fork.

Ben had one deformed hand but nevertheless had developed skilful ways of managing to do most things for himself. He also quickly learnt it was best to behave around staff, ever since the day he kicked nurse Mandy in the shin. Following the incident, as the staff called it, he'd had small privileges taken away. In his heart, Ben knew she deserved it, because he saw what Mandy did to Linny and heard those awful words: 'If you don't stop scratching in the dirt, you filthy chook, I'll pull your fingernails out.' The nurse swiftly pulled Linny up from the ground and hosed her hands and nails until the little girl screamed. Ben's roommates had previously told him of another boy who once had his fingernails pulled out. He wasn't sure if it was true or not, because the boy was no longer and inpatient on the island. Thinking worse things might happen to Linny and in a moment of rage to protect her, Ben lashed out and kicked Mandy hard in the leg.

'Little bugger,' Mandy yelled at Ben. 'Santa won't be coming to you!' She let go of Linny and called to one of the male nurses to restrain Ben.

After a few days without privileges, such as going for walks outside the ward fence, or watching TV, Ben divulged his worries one evening to his preferred nurse, Rick. He told how Mandy had threatened Linny. Rick tended to believe Ben and promised he would look into it. He also set some goals for Ben to help him regain back his privileges. Firstly, Ben would need to say sorry to the nurse for kicking and then undertake some small tasks in exchange for tokens.

Rick further reassured Ben. 'In the end, it will work in your favour. I know it's hard for you here, but somehow we all just have to get along.'

The jobs of picking up the newspapers and sweeping the veranda were a small price to pay, and Ben easily earned the required tokens to have his privileges restored.

Smiling at Rick, he announced, 'Will Santa now bring me a present?'

Rick patted the boy on the back. 'Of course he will. Santa never misses anyone,' he said. turning his head to hide his misty eyes.

On Christmas Day. the sunshine glistened over the Hawkesbury River as if someone had thrown a handful of diamonds. The cicada chorus screeched so loud it almost drowned out the Jingle Bells music when the children awoke.

'Merry Christmas!' Rick cheered when each of the boys rose.

'Are you Santa?' a boy called, pointing to Rick's red hat with a white pompom.

'No. I'm one of the helpers,' he grinned. 'Once you're all up and dressed and we've had breakfast, then we'll see what presents Santa brought.'

'How did he get here? We haven't got a chimney in this ward,' one of the older boys said with a hint of disbelief.

'He came on a riverboat and unloaded at Mooney Mooney. Early in the morning, the night nurse told me he heard the clatter of reindeer hooves pulling the sleigh across the causeway onto the island.' Rick winked at the boy.

The older boy smiled watching the little one's faces light up. 'I forgot. Santa always comes that way.'

*

It was surprising, even to Mandy, how quick and painless it was getting the children ready for the day – even Linny stayed inside away from the garden until the gift opening began. One less time she'd have to scrub the girl's fingernails, Mandy thought, especially since her mother was coming for lunch.

Opening the mountain of presents was the highlight of the morning. Each child vigorously ripped the paper from the packages handed out by Rick. Ben, like most of the others, received a couple of new T-shirts and a cardboard stocking with stretchy red gauze on the outside, so trinkets and lollies could be stored and carried around. Santa also brought Ben a small fishing rod labelled with his name. It would be left in the ward office for safekeeping until he was taken to the jetty to go fishing. Along with the other boys, Ben received a soccer ball and a water pistol – always fun on a hot day – and some other items, which were labelled and secured away. The girls received dolls, hair clips, tiny soaps and new undies – some with coloured patterns. Linny's most beloved item was a new swimming cossie, which she wouldn't let go of for the entire morning. There were also some presents left by Santa for the whole ward, including new ping-pong bats and balls, a couple of picnic things such as rugs, a portable cassette player for music and a bait and tackle box.

Late morning, a handful of relatives started arriving.

Rosa inhaled the fresh country air when she approached the large brick buildings. Set amongst the tranquil scenery of gums and flowering grevilleas along the sandy river bays, the island refuge belied what lay inside. The rabble of children in the ward provided a stark contrast. It was a relief to Rosa, though, to see the pastel-painted hallways and walls dotted with a bit more colour from Christmas cards and sparkling tinsel draped over doorways. Rosa noted how few relatives had visited for the thirty kids in the ward – only about half a dozen.

The children who had no visitors tended to hover close by to another child's family member. Invariably, these visitors knew to bring a few small gifts or lollies to share among the kids and they didn't seem to mind others milling around them for a hug.

This overt demonstration of wanting to belong to someone touched the hearts of many staff. Rick noticed even Mandy had a smile on her face, perhaps because she knew she could eventually hand Linny over – clean for once – to her mother for an hour or so. This was the usual amount of time the relatives stayed before they needed to move on, bidding farewell with 'Sorry, must go…can't miss the next train, need to get home to cook dinner, must get to see my mother and other children later…'

All was progressing well until lunchtime. The feeding frenzy, dribbling, spluttering and face wiping was something Mandy found disgusting. On many occasions, she had complained to Rick, 'Why can't we eat first? It's enough to turn me off my food.' As the manager, he often gave in to her whingeing and allocated her other chores to attend to while he and the rest of the staff presided over mealtimes.

At one of the tables, each of about eight people, sat Linny's mother Rosa, with her daughter on one side and Ben on the other. Some other children sat opposite with one other adult visitor. After pulling the Christmas bonbons and putting on paper hats, the adults and the bigger boys read out the corny jokes and laughed, whether they understood or not.

Linny giggled and scrunched her red paper hat, which sat skew-whiff on her head. Her dress and fingernails, her mother noticed, were clean.

Rosa smiled, stroked her now cropped, shiny hair and hugged her.

Linny grinned back. 'Mmmmmm…mmmm.'

Rosa wasn't quite sure if it was a murmur or hum. Either way, she cherished the notion that Linny had voiced Mum.

The kitchen staff served a hot meal, typical of Australian Christmas fare at the time, even in ninety-degree Fahrenheit heat. There were plenty of baked potatoes, pumpkin and gravy to accompany the roast chicken, pork and other vegetables. The kids were usually made to eat their green vegetables first, but the staff turned a blind eye at Christmas. Hence, the potatoes were quickly gobbled up.

Rosa cut up her daughter's food and clasped one of Linny's claw-like hands, which she'd been busy scratching the table with. Rosa was delighted to see Linny was managing to grip a fork, ready to stab food with her other hand, though intermittently she bent over her plate and pecked at pieces with her mouth, usually when the effort of feeding herself was getting a bit slow.

Ben beamed at Linny's mother and held out his deformed hand. 'I taught Linny to eat with a fork. She copied me.'

'Good boy, Ben. You've done well.'

The chicken was more difficult for Linny to pierce with the fork.

After a few failed attempts at missing the drumstick, the older boy opposite started to laugh. 'Look at Linny,' he sniggered to the boy next to him. 'She's eating herself! Linny's a chook…Linny's a chook,' he chanted while rocking on his chair.

Outraged at the unkindness towards her daughter, Rosa's face reddened. Meanwhile, Linny flung her fork across the table, barely missing the father of another girl. Ben rushed to find Rick, who having heard the kerfuffle, arrived in an instant to intervene. The fight was soon broken up and the children separated and taken away from the table. Rosa clutched her daughter's hand and proceeded to the basin to wash her.

Rick, secretly grateful no one was physically hurt, called to Mandy to come into the dining room to help settle Linny and clean up the food she'd smeared over herself and matted through her hair.

Scanning the mess, Mandy huffed through the door and hissed to her colleague when she passed. 'I told you Linny is an animal.'

Overhearing those last few words, Linny's mother's eyes brimmed over. 'It's what her father said when he locked her in the chook yard,' Rosa choked, 'but she's still mine and I love her.'

Neptune's Necklace

Clem Dawson stirred at five a.m., woken by a howling wind. The east coast low had intensified overnight and it was now blowing like the clappers. Instinctively, he reached across the bed for his wife Minnie. The sheet was cold.

He then remembered their argument the evening before. Minnie wanted fresh fish for dinner and Clem's tired bones didn't relish the thought of traipsing down to the bay and unhitching the small rowboat to go fishing. He was aware there was a low-pressure system developing offshore from Victoria, which always meant a storm exploded into gale force winds and plenty of rain.

During the previous evening, Clem settled in at home to enjoy a few whiskies washed down with beer in front of the open fire in his beach hut. Meanwhile, Minnie banged on about bloody fish. He must have fallen asleep.

At half past five in the morning, at first light, Clem was ready to get going. He dressed and threw on his moleskin jacket. The sun was just about to peep over the horizon. Reaching the shoreline, he found his wooden boat smashed about, but still tied with its rope tether tied to a fallen tree.

Standing akimbo, Clem stared into the vast expanse of the bay. He knew every inch of it after fifty years of living on the shoreline. He knew the tides, the rocks, the shoals and sandbanks which created the waves and swelled in a big storm. He knew the likely places where a body would wash up.

Minutes later, a police car rounded the bend, illuminating the gravel road. It stopped short of knocking Clem over.

'What's up? Lost something?' the officer shouted.

Clem recognised the voice – always bloody Constable Duncan Hodges. Clem had known him since the death of his first wife Eliza, who'd been discovered not far from where he was now, drowned and washed up on the sand twenty years ago.

Clem scanned the bay, watching ripples of wind gusting on the breeze line. He wiped salt spray from his face and stinging eyes with the back of his hand before answering. 'Maybe. Minnie didn't come home last night. She wanted to go fishing – heard the big dhufish were running.' Clem left it at that, preferring Duncan to dig for information.

'And?'

'The rowboat's back but no sign of her,' Clem answered.

'Not a good time to go out in this weather. By the way, your neighbours called last night. Said there was a bit of a barney going on in your shack.'

Clem grimaced at the idea of the nosy neighbours interfering in his business. 'Yes, Duncan! We had a few words. I told Minnie it was stupid to want to go fishing and the wind would blow a dog off its chain. Then I had a few grogs and fell asleep. Just woke now.'

'When do you think she went? How long's she been out there?'

'How would I bloody well know?'

A pesky pelican, wings sodden from the rain, flapped and snapped at Clem's legs. He knew it was Pippy, Minnie's favourite pelican who she fed fish to every day. Clem attempted to kick the bird away, a gesture which did not unnoticed by Duncan.

'Is that Pippy?'

'Yeah. Dumb bird. Must be wanting Minnie's fish scraps.'

'Seems a pretty smart bird to me, mate. I think we'd better organise a search.'

'Thanks, Duncan, that would be helpful, but I think I know these waters and the shoreline better than any of your young coppers.'

'Even so, I'll call a few in. You better get back inside.'

Clem dawdled slowly towards his house. He turned when the police car was out of sight and headed back to the beach to cut the tether from the boat, all the while praying Duncan hadn't seen the rope. He then began his own search, hoping he'd find Minnie before anyone else.

Trudging through the soggy sand, Clem reminisced about happier days long ago when he and Eliza sunbaked on the beach. His first wife loved to collect debris of seashells and driftwood. She especially liked long strands of sea grapes or bubble weed. Clem told her its real name was Neptune's necklace. He showed her how she looked with a strand strung together around her neck. When Eliza sat on the sand, Clem buried her feet and legs up to her knees and took a photo.

'My lovely mermaid,' Clem said, and they both laughed.

Those days alone as a couple didn't last, because it wasn't long before Minnie, Eliza's friend who was a couple of years younger, began to frequently join them. Minnie also liked to pretend to be mermaids. Before Eliza's drowning, a myriad of photos was taken of them together over the years, which now adorned the walls of their beach shack.

Clem's reverie was broken when he heard footsteps scrunching through the washed-up sticks and seaweed. He then saw the cops combing the shore around the bend in the bay, which had created a natural breakwater leading into the mouth of the river tributary.

'Think we've found her, Duncan,' a young police officer called.

En masse, the officers diverged onto the spot where a mound of washed-up debris had been swept into the mouth of the river. Beneath the seaweed and bits of old wood and plastic boat fenders, a shoe was visible on a leg sticking out. The face of Minnie appeared, bloated and unrecognisable. Her mouth was stuffed with dangling sea grass.

Pippy appeared in no time and began snapping and pecking at Minnie's body.

Clem raced to the scene. 'Get that bloody pelican away,' he growled.

He looked down at the face of his second wife, pale, cold and scraggly haired. Her two left hand fingers were caught in her Neptune's necklace, now plumped with seawater and a pale yellowish-green. Leaning over, using his body to cover her face, Clem furtively slipped Minnie's fingers out and attempted to pull her up.

Constable Hodges tapped him on the shoulder. 'I'm sorry, Clem. It looks like she gulped water in the big swell and swallowed a mouthful of weed which clogged in her throat.'

Clem nodded, speechless.

'A bit of *déjà vu*, don't you think, Clem?'

Again, Clem said nothing. He glared at Duncan.

'Sorry, mate, but we'll have to take her body away for the coroner.'

Clem nodded once more when the police officers cordoned off the scene and arranged for the transfer of Minnie's body.

With hands stuffed into his pockets, Clem nodded to Constable Duncan and headed home when the ambulance left with Minnie. He walked away and fiddled with the bubble weed in his right hand, squeezing each sea grape until it popped. By the time Clem reached his beach shack, his pocket was drenched.

The neighbours, who'd been gawking at the whole scenario, stopped him to say a few words. 'Sorry, Clem, to hear about Minnie. Let us know if we can do anything.'

Clem clenched his hidden fists and grunted. He wanted to say, 'Keep your noses out of my business,' but he didn't. Sometimes it was best to keep your mouth shut – like he did after Eliza's death.

Clem's tactic of silence worked. However, the flipside was that the neighbours and a lot of the other townsfolk nattered for years about what might really have happened. Doubting faces had glared at him in the pub. As well, the local paper sometimes did a piece following up on drownings in an attempt to create a warning every time a big storm threatened. What really flared the suspicion of some people was the day Clem married Minnie, just over a year from losing his first wife.

In the end, Clem kept much to himself, his best friend being the bottle of Glenfiddich he received every year from his old mate in Sydney, who dropped by on his way to Coffs Harbour for Christmas with his own family. After Clem finished the bottle, he was then onto cheaper varieties for the rest of the year.

Mostly, Clem kept his drinking sessions until after dinner. He and Minnie led a somewhat secluded life and rubbed along harmoniously by day. Late in the evening, though, things escalated when they fought constantly, each raising their voice to outdo the other.

The neighbours often complained about the commotion, yet when they saw Minnie feed Pippy each morning, they lavished all their sympathy towards her. 'Bad one last night, luv? You poor thing. Don't know how you put up with such a cranky old sea dog.'

Minnie lapped up their kindness, ready to use the words against her husband when their next fight erupted.

Clem's usual way to end an argument was to warn his second wife, 'If I were you, Minnie, I'd keep away from those gossips. You never know when they might turn on you.'

Those words usually gave rise to the couple sleeping in separate beds. Nonetheless, all seemed sunny again by morning, when Minnie would cook a big breakfast of scrambled eggs with a mountain of fresh rock oysters on the side.

Days later, when the news of Minnie's drowning was finally off the front page of the local paper, Clem heard his gate squeak open. Straining to look out of his salt-sprayed opaque window, he saw Duncan accompanied by an older man and a young female uniformed officer. It always amazed him how anyone entering his home could negotiate their way through the junk he'd collected without tripping. Eventually, the police constable knocked on the door. The local coroner looked pale and wrinkled, probably not much better than half the bodies he'd dealt with in the morgue, Clem thought, stifling a chuckle. Breathless, the older man was ushered inside and introduced when he plonked himself on the couch. Duncan then announced his young officer, Sandy Winters.

'Nice to meet you, Mr Dawson.' Sandy offered her hand to shake. 'It's certainly a sizeable collection you have out there.'

Strewn across the path were driftwood logs and strung from the trees were old fishing nets with corks at regular intervals along the edges. Washed-up mooring buoys – orange, white and barnacled – hung like giant Christmas baubles. Strings of sticks and seashells rattled in the breeze at the entrance to the split timber shack.

'Hope you like it. The backyard's even more interesting. I call it art and my Minnie called it beach craft. The neighbours don't seem to like it, though. They said my house looked worse than the local tip – always complaining to the council to get me to clean it up.'

'Well, Clem, you have to admit it is a bit of a fire hazard,' Duncan said.

Prompting Duncan to move on, the coroner coughed.

'Anyway, Clem, we're here to discuss other matters. Sandy, would you mind getting us a glass of water while we get the paperwork sorted?'

Sandy responded to his cue. 'Sure, no worries.' She sensed Duncan wanted to her have a quick stickybeak in case there was anything they'd missed, while he started the conversation with Clem.

The coroner spoke first. 'Mr Dawson, I'm sorry to hear about your wife's death. As you are aware, we needed to do a thorough examination to find out the exact cause of death.'

'And?' Clem started fiddling in his pocket.

'Well, at this point, I can only give you a preliminary finding of accidental drowning and asphyxiation, after swallowing seaweed.'

'Not much more than we expected, Clem,' Duncan said. 'However, it doesn't mean we've finished the case.'

Clem tilted his head towards the coroner, who added, 'We've taken blood and tissue samples and a complete set of photos. We will need to wait a few weeks before the toxicology report comes back, along with other diagnostics from body tissue, and also the seaweed and any other items found on your wife's body.'

Duncan resumed questioning Clem about any drugs, alcohol or other things Minnie was taking which might come up in the toxicology report.

Clem gave him a quizzical glance and then answered honestly that he was unaware of anything she took, except for a small aspirin daily and a few vitamins.

Sandy re-entered the room and handed out the drinks. 'Sorry it took a while, but I saw those ripe lemons out the kitchen window and had to climb up to pick a few for the water.'

'Thanks, Sandy, tastes great.' Duncan sipped his drink and gestured to the coroner to wrap up.

'So, Mr Dawson, at this stage as I said, the results are only preliminary and dependent upon further tests. But at the moment we have all we need, so we can release your wife's body for her funeral.'

Duncan stood and the others followed. 'By the way, Clem, you know where we are. If there's anything you think to tell us about that night, don't hesitate to come down to the station.'

Glad to see the back of the trio, Clem closed the door and headed for his whisky bottle.

Once they'd dropped the coroner back at his workplace, the two police officers stopped at a bakery for a takeaway coffee and finger bun.

Sandy was twitchy, ready to talk to Duncan. 'I think I've found something, a bit weird, yet it seems connected with the case.'

Duncan raised his hand. 'Hang on, just wait – can't think straight without my caffeine.'

After they had both had a few sips and Duncan seemed settled, Sandy began.

'I had a quick snoop around the backyard, which was like Clem said, very interesting. Well, to arty people maybe, but it looked an even bigger a mess than the front yard to me. Then I smelt something like fresh paint. I turned my head towards the narrow side path near the kitchen window.'

'I agree, it is weird,' Duncan interrupted. 'The paint smell, I mean – the place hasn't had a lick of paint for twenty years. Go on.'

'Hidden from direct view by a lattice-covered vine were three small wooden crosses. The first one was very old and difficult to read, but I made out the word Eliza. There were some dates I couldn't quite decipher.'

'Probably her birth and death dates. It was about twenty years ago.'

'A line was written underneath the dates in black flaking paint. It said, "My lovely Mermaid." What would that mean?'

Duncan grinned. 'Funny old bugger, Clem. Years ago, he used to take photos of her, and then Minnie, on the beach covered to their knees in the sand with seaweed hair…'

'That's it!'

'What?'

Eager to tell her version, Sandy felt she was now onto something. 'There was a necklace of weed on each of the women's graves. You know the stuff. It gets washed up all the time. When I was a kid, we used to pop the little beads until they squirted.'

'I do know it. I think that was part of the women's mermaid attire.'

'It's more than that, Duncan. On Eliza's cross, the necklace was broken and crackly. It was dried out after many years, yet it still held together.'

'What with?'

'Fishing line, thick like the stuff with a good breaking strain to catch big fish. I only saw it because the necklace was disintegrating. So I checked the new cross, the one for Minnie. The dates of birth and death were clear, and a fresh necklace made from the same stuff hung there. I couldn't see the fishing line because the weed was so thick and plump. The line was intertwined close against the weed, so I felt for it – definitely there.'

Duncan seemed deep in thought. 'A bit suspicious, don't you think?'

'There could have been foul play. Maybe they both were strangled with the necklaces. There's no way fishing line so strong would break.'

'I agree, Sandy. We'll check out the photos and I'll investigate Eliza's death certificate. When we have more evidence, it'll be time to bring Clem in to explain. Might even ask him who the other cross is for.'

'Sorry, I nearly forgot, one more thing. On Minnie's grave, the words "My mortal Mermaid" were written in black.'

Clem half expected Constable Duncan and his officer Sandy to pay him another visit soon. He was waiting for them when they arrived at his front door a few days later.

'Clem, we need you to come down to the station,' Duncan said.

Feigning a puzzled look, Clem asked, 'What for?'

'I think you might know, mate,' Duncan said.

Reluctantly, Clem strolled to the car with his listing gait – a bit like an old ship holed in the side and slowly sinking.

From the time they left in the car and arrived at the police station, Clem had been trembling and muttering to himself. He was taken to the interview room while Sandy and Duncan collected the evidence and other requirements for the session.

Sandy spoke softly to Duncan when they approached the interview room. 'What is it he keeps mumbling about? Sounds like singing mermaids.'

Duncan picked up on it up straight away. 'Just an old T.S. Eliot poem we used to learn about at school in my day. The line is "I have heard the mermaids singing, each to each. / I do not think that they will sing to me."'

'What does it mean?'

'I think he's referring to his two wives – they were thick as thieves at times and caused a lot of trouble for him. Anyway, best get on with the interview.'

Clem raised his head when the officers entered the room.

Duncan spoke. 'Clem, you're now arrested and under suspicion of murder for your wife Minnie Dawson and also for the involvement in the drowning of your first wife Eliza.'

There was no reaction from Clem, so Duncan continued. 'We have found forensic evidence of strangulation with fishing line, intertwined in the Neptune's necklace each was wearing, and small abrasions on the neck and under the fingernails of Minnie's left hand. We also have old photographic evidence showing the same sort of strangulation with Eliza. We believe the necklaces hanging on the two crosses were used in the killings. They are currently being seized for further examination. Do you have anything to add?'

Shaky, Clem continued mumbling.

'Just tell us the truth.'

'You think I'd kill Eliza. I loved her and would have stayed with her forever, if it wasn't for Minnie and their stupid mermaid games.'

Duncan added, 'I do remember those days, Clem, and agree both the women were a bit out of control then – even turning up half drunk at the local Christmas pageant in their skin-tight sequinned fishtail costumes.'

Clem's eyes crinkled at the corners and he held back a smile. 'Yeah, they even had their stinking Neptune's necklaces on and…'

'Well, are you guilty as charged?' Duncan prompted.

'No bloody way. I told you, I loved Eliza. It was Minnie who killed her. She was jealous and they both got raging drunk one night and took the rowboat out. I was asleep. The story I heard the next morning from Minnie was apparently a big squall blasted through – though I didn't hear it – and they started arguing in the boat. The fight was about me.'

Clem paused when he noticed an inquisitive look on Sandy's face. 'I know it's hard to believe, but it was the way it was. You wouldn't think two women would fall for an old bugger like me. Anyway, Eliza slapped Minnie and a physical fight broke out. Minnie said the boat rocked and Eliza nearly slipped overboard, so she grabbed her by the necklace and held on tight. In effect, she was strangling Eliza, who after a couple of minutes, now a dead weight, fell into the bay and quickly drifted away. Anyhow, that was Minnie's story. My lovely mermaid floated into shore on the morning tide…and you know the rest.'

Duncan sighed, not sure if he totally believed Clem's version of Minnie's story, aware of her wild moods at times. 'If that's the case with Eliza, then who killed Minnie?'

'It was me. After Eliza's death I felt sorry for Minnie. She had nowhere to go and despaired about what had happened to Eliza. Maybe she wasn't telling the whole truth. Anyway, I grew fond of her. She needed protection, so I married her and promised not to say anything about Eliza's drowning to anyone. It was an attempt to stop the town gossip.' Tears welled in Clem's eyes, and he hung his head low and began muttering once more.

'Go on, Clem.'

'I loved and hated Minnie at the same time…but in the end the bad days outweighed the good. We quarrelled the evening of her death about going fishing. The weather was blowing up a gale. I relented and said I'd take her out for an hour only, after dusk. Once out there, she didn't want to turn back, even though the storm was imminent. We argued more, of course. She threatened me with a fish knife. I struggled to take it off her, defending myself. Then something snapped. I grabbed her bloody Neptune's necklace and did the same to her as she had done to my Eliza. Now they're together and I can finally have a bit of peace.'

'The third cross – who is it for?' Duncan asked.

'Me of course. Haven't got long to go after seeing the doc last week – couple of months at the most.' Clem seemed relieved and his taut facial muscles relaxed. 'Do what you need to, Duncan. Quite frankly, I'm looking forward to my death. Just hope those two aren't where I'm going.' He chuckled and murmured. 'My mermaids sing…but not to me.'

Ice

'Another ice addict on the warpath,' Lena overheard the nurse sigh to a colleague upon entering St Vincent's Hospital on Saturday morning to visit a friend.

There had been a kerfuffle in the emergency department after a young man punched a security guard in the gut, leaving him winded. The lad continued to strut, swearing at things not there for others to see. Threatening to kill the next person who came near him, his wild eyes and unruly red hair caused a mother to cower protecting her small infant. An elderly man looked away until more security arrived. Eventually, with help from the local coppers, they grabbed and led the youth outside and away from the hospital.

Once sent on his way, the lad raved and spluttered obscenities. Just another weekend on the streets of Darlinghurst, Sydney. Methamphetamine or crystal meth, commonly called ice because of its chunky clear crystals, is readily available these days.

Later, after visiting, Lena left via the back entrance to walk to her car. The same young man she'd seen earlier was now more settled yet still muttering incoherently. The lad fidgeted with a broken buckle on his leather sandal, while lying on the grass verge of Barcom Avenue. His eyes seemed fixated on the sandstone wall, which led into a laneway. Lena wondered who he was waiting for, maybe a mate, or his dealer. She followed his gaze to a sunlit sign, Ice Street. What a strange name. A bit of a coincidence considering the changes over many years, nowadays reflective of some people who frequent the area. She decided to research the laneway's history.

*

Home at last, trudging with six bags of grocery shopping, Lena plonked the bags on the back porch and fiddled for her door key. Then she saw it. 'Damn, not again.'

She'd overwatered the hardy peace lily – the only thing she seemed to be able to grow. Muddy water leaked onto the tiles. The tiles weren't the problem, though; it was leaking onto the old icebox where the plant sat. The antique wooden ice chest had survived in her family for a hundred years. Its pale wood was scrubbed back and sealed, and the brass latches polished. No longer in use, the inside of the metal case was left to anodise with age. The drowned plant seeped dark-brownish stains down the exterior. It was once a family treasure. So small on its four swivel wheels, slightly above waist height, with two doors. The bottom door opened outward to reveal a wire-rack shelf. The top hatch lifted upward into a metal sealed area. The brass plate read 'Freezesi'.

Lena remembered using the icebox at the family holiday house. With no extra fridge in the 1950s, it came in handy. The gloved iceman delivered block-ice twice weekly, which he plopped into the top area with heavy metal tongs. Melting ice-water drained and dripped through the veranda floorboards. The ice block only lasted long enough to keep essentials cool in the bottom section, not big by today's standards of the mega-fridge, yet big enough for milk, butter, the day's catch, and bottles of Reschs beer standing upright when the wire shelf was removed. Lena recalled her grandmother telling her about people who delivered food, including the Fisho, Rabbitoh, Milko and whoever butchered fresh meat.

Opening the back door, she grabbed a rag to soak up the mess, before the family noticed she'd once again overwatered the peace lily, which didn't exude any calmness.

Inside the kitchen, Lena unpacked fridge and freezer items into compartmentalised spaces. She pondered how people managed in days gone by. Keeping food fresh for a large family, in small ice chests and always being reliant on the iceman to deliver before food perished, wouldn't have been easy. Her ancestors must have led a precarious existence making sure no one died of food poisoning from smelly fish or greying rabbits. Tough and resilient, they utilised various forms of water cooling as a breeze blew through muslin cloth, along with fly-screened pantries. They helped until the ice came. But where did the iceman get the ice? Why didn't it melt while transported across the countryside?

*

The following Saturday, Lena googled the name of the laneway, aptly called Ice Street around 1860, when an ice-making factory was established. A tiny name for a big achievement. James Harrison, from Melbourne, found a novel way to make ice using ammonia gas instead of ether. His method enabled the recapture of evaporated ammonia, by turning it back into liquid in a cyclical manner. This became the crucial factor in making ice affordable. Ice Street was known then as 'the Birth of Refrigeration'. Harrison's simpler method was less costly than bringing sawn chunks of winter ice wrapped in sawdust, in ship's holds from North American lakes.

*

Another rainy evening, Lena set out again to visit St Vinnie's. The traffic was horrendous. Impatient drivers honked their horns and slammed their brakes, barely missing other cars. She was glad to finally stop. The back laneway seemed very different from the previous week. Rain had driven everyone indoors. Lights dazzled and glistened through downpours. Sirens wailed their way into the emergency bay.

An ambulance stopped as she approached the hospital doors. A trolley unloaded to meet staff waiting for their next critical victim, on what looked like escalating into a busy shift.

'Unconscious. Ice OD,' the ambo called through the ruckus to the receiving medic.

A sheet-covered man, except for his head and a leather-sandalled foot, was ventilated via a tube attached to oxygen, manned by paramedics. Things looked grim. A flash of red hair caught Lena's eye when the patient was whisked inside for resus. The image of the lad's face image from the week before returned.

Lena imagined the perils of keeping food fresh long ago, without ice. 'Is life any less risky or hazardous now?' she asked herself, after seeing the damage done to drug users and others by another type of 'ice'. The three-letter street name had certainly retained its relevance after one hundred and fifty years.

The Gelato Bar

'Whatcha' lookin' at, blind boy?' the customer provoked, while his mates sniggered in the background.

They were hoping to watch Mike squirm, or at least see his face redden. They saw neither.

Mike, who was soaking up the late afternoon sun's rays on his Polaroid lenses, snapped out of his reverie. Mike replied. 'Yeah, yeah, heard that one before. Now what would you like?' Steadying himself with two hands on the ledge of the chilly counter, he awaited their onslaught – a taunting game the gang of local louts played when attempting to trick him into making a mistake.

The gang leader shot first. 'I'll have a double cone with rum and raisin on the bottom and topped with mango.'

The second voice sounded in quick succession. 'Give me a cup with two spoons, thanks. Boysenberry, choc ripple and a scoop of vanilla.'

Then another. A sweeter voice this time. 'Lemon sorbet for me, with cookies and cream and a few nuts on top.'

'Cup or cone?'

The girl hesitated and batted eyelids Mike could not see. 'Oh, I'm not sure. What do you suggest, Mikey?'

A hint of a smile illuminated his face. 'Maybe a cup so the nuts don't fall off.'

'Come on, mate, hurry up. I ordered before her,' the first boy shouted. He glanced at the girl. 'Anyway, you know blind boy only has eyes for one girl.' His mates sniggered again at their ringleader's pun.

'Okay, slow down, guys, I'll get there.'

Mike breathed through his nostrils to smell the scent of the different ice cream flavours. Luckily, the counter of the gelato bar at the end of his uncle's cafe was small. There were only twelve tubs, six in each row. Ever since the recent accident when he had lost his sight, Mike honed his memory for many things, and the placement of the tubs was critical to his part-time holiday job, where he could still imagine the pastel colours of the ice cream.

The front row from Mike's right to left held Mango, Vanilla, Strawberry, Honeycomb, Lemon sorbet and Caramel. The back row closest to the cones and scoopers consisted of Butterscotch, Choc ripple, Boysenberry, Rum and Raisin, Cookies and Cream and Macadamia.

Each tub sported a little flag on a stick rammed into the gelato so the customers could choose. These flags meant nothing to Mike and were put in position by the café manager who set up each day. One time, however, to Mike's bamboozlement and embarrassment, a couple of the flags had been incorrectly placed. Some newer customers quickly became impatient. Ever since the fiasco, Mike had double-checked the set-up and learnt to associate the tub positions from their smell.

After four hours of intense concentration, Mike was relieved when the manager let him off fifteen minutes early. The manager had seen the gang return twice in the evening to heckle, so offered to do the clean-up, enabling Mike to get away when his older brother Henry called in to pick him up.

At home, Mike and Henry plonked themselves at either end of a scratchy horsehair couch on the veranda of their riverside home. Their parents had wanted to get rid of the tatty sofa, but the boys were determined to keep it. Each had their own end with an ashtray on the arms where they downed a couple of beers and smoked Drum rollies, and sometimes a joint, before heading to bed.

Mike gazed across the water to the northern shore at a formidable three-storey house with an octagonal turret atop. His eyes could no longer see the tiny front window at the peak of the turret. This was where Cassie would stand and look across at the two boys who, more often than not, were fiddling in their waterfront cave with bits of boats, kayaks and fishing gear.

'Mike, she's not there any more.'

'I know, Henry, but she did say she'd come back.'

'Well, you can't see over there anyway, so there's no use staring for hours on end. Come on, let's call it a night.'

'Think I'll wait a bit longer.'

'Okay, but remember tomorrow we're up early because your HSC exam results are coming out – and Mum's taking you to the eye doctor later in the day.'

'Sure. Won't be long.'

Mike still couldn't break his habit of watching the turret for a glimpse of Cassie. It seemed like he'd done it all his life. Mike's day-dreaming transported him back to when he was about eight years old, when he caught sight of a thick plaited yellow rope hanging from the turret window. He'd grabbed his father's binoculars and took a closer look. Cassie and her friend Anna, who lived in the mansion below, were hanging out the window laughing as they swung the plait.

At the time, he and Henry had been playing pirate games. Mike quickly urged his brother to untie the tinny so they could motor across the river and investigate what the girls were up to. Arriving near the other shore, they'd heard them giggle and chant, 'Rapunzel, let down your golden hair.' The boys immediately cut the engine of the small boat and tossed out the anchor into a sandy inlet. Ever since they connected, the four children had spent many hours toing and froing across the river playing silly pirate games exploring the foreshores. Inevitably, the boys would end up dropping the girls at Anna's house before eating a carton of choc-chip ice cream between them. Later, in their early teens, these pastimes gradually morphed into awkward fondling and kisses. It was a year or so later when the girls and boys paired off – Anna and Henry with their matching rock-pool eyes, and Cassie and Mike, she with green eyes and his smoky-blue.

Mike smiled to himself at the memory of those childhood days. He went to sleep convinced it was from the very first day he saw the yellow plait from the turret window when he fell in love with Cassie.

*

Meanwhile, the day before the exam results were published, Cassie was fidgeting in the kitchen at her grandparents' property in Armidale, when her mother spoke.

'How about you go for a walk, Cass, get some of that energy out, or you'll be tossing and turning all night until you get those results.'

'Good idea, Mum, think I will. Anyhow, it's in the lap of the gods now.'

'Well, what's worrying you then?'

'I'm looking forward to talking to Mike again. We made a pact when I left to come up here – we'd wait until we got our results before we contacted each other.'

'So what's the problem? You'll talk with him tomorrow.'

'He was supposed to see me in the evening before us leaving at the crack of dawn to drive up here. He didn't show up and never gave me a reason. I can't believe he's forgotten me.'

Cassie's mother sought to provide a simple explanation. 'We did have to get away early after your last exam. He was probably caught up celebrating with his mates and drank too much.'

'I'm…worried.' Cassie strained to hold back the mistiness in her eyes. However, when her mum hugged her the tears were as inescapable as a run-out tide. 'I think maybe he's found someone else.'

'Why? You two have been together nearly your whole life. I've seen the way he looks at you. Cass, he adores you.'

'I spoke to Anna the other day and she seemed a bit abrupt. Wouldn't talk about what Mike was up to. Just blabbed on about her and Henry getting a flat together after she starts uni. You know she hopes to get into medicine so she can be in the same faculty as him.'

'Come on, we'll walk together,' Cassie's mother said as she linked arms, fearing a break-up with Mike would break her daughter's heart.

The following morning began as a typical day in the rural community. Everyone was up early with chores to do, chickens to feed, eggs to collect and cows to milk. Cassie's grandma had a cooked breakfast of

French toast and bacon ready, so they could head to town early to buy the newspaper with the exam results as soon as it arrived in town.

'Come on, Cass, let's go,' her mum said, gulping her last mouthful of strong Bushells tea.

'Can I drive, Mum?'

'Sure, the more experience you have now before you get your licence the better, especially if you're accepted into teachers college in Armidale and need to commute.'

Cassie felt a lump in her throat and just nodded, unable to reply. She knew her mother, as a single mum, had given up a lot by taking on piecework sewing which she could do from their small turret, in order to provide her daughter with a good education. Nevertheless, Cassie also realised her grandparents were ageing and also needed her mother's help on the farm. It was a dilemma Cassie tossed about before she would eventually face her decision. Even if she did get into uni or a teachers college, she had hoped to do her degree in the city. She had hoped to stay near Mike.

Back in Sydney, a sliver of sunshine crept up behind the Harbour Bridge. The city glowed. Anna woke early to get the newspaper to view her results, confident she'd done well, enabling her to matriculate into any university and any subject she chose. Henry was fetching her on his way, as he was taking Mike to get his results. They could both celebrate together.

The thought of Mike's accident, immediately after the final HSC exam, still sent a stab of pain through Anna. She shivered at the thought of Mike having to tell Cassie how his life had irrevocably changed.

A horn beeped from the road. Time to go – which meant it would soon be time for Mike to make a call to Cassie.

The HSC exam outcomes were as expected. Anna squealed with delight seeing her name as first in the state for science, along with excellent grades in all subjects, which meant she'd matriculated into medicine at Sydney Uni to be with Henry, who'd just completed his second year there. She also noticed from the published results that Cassie had done well and earned good marks, enough to get into any teachers college she chose. Anna decided to call later in the morning to congratulate her.

Mike seemed a bit down and really didn't care how well he'd done. It was of no consequence now whether his marks were good or bad. His lack of sight meant there was no way he could study engineering at UNSW. As it happened, he did get the results needed, yet showed no joy when he slunk away with Henry through the gathering groups of eighteen-year-olds discussing their grades. Mike continued walking, fussing with his sunglasses, making sure they covered his eye patches.

'Well done! I knew your hard work would pay off,' Henry said.

'Yeah, got what I expected, but it doesn't mean much now.'

Henry wrapped his arm across Mike's shoulder, temporarily choked while trying to the right response. He gathered himself and said, 'You know, Mike, life's not over. I'm with you every step of the way. We'll sort this out. Are you going to ring Cassie?'

'A bit later…not sure what to say right now. Think I'll go home for a bit and ring her after my eye appointment.'

'Okay, but you know Anna's going to talk to her soon, so what do you suggest she says to Cass?'

'Just tell her I went well, got the results I expected, but I can't ring her for a couple of hours. Make up some excuse we have to help our dad with something.'

At home, Mike relaxed once more and sat at his end of the veranda couch. His head automatically swerved towards the turret on the opposite riverbank. *How can I tell you, Cassie, our future is not what we expected…and I don't want you to waste yours spending it with me?*

Mike shook his head to clear his mind and he rehashed the events of the evening a couple of months ago. Involuntarily, he shivered. It was the night of the accident. Around eleven p.m., he'd just arrived home, a bit under the weather, after more than a few beers with his mates celebrating the end of exams. He was desperate to catch up with Cassie before she left early to go to her grandparents' Armidale farm. He'd made a promise to see her and wasn't about to break it.

Wobbling, Mike attempted to launch himself into the tinny. The moon was half-full covered with a little cloud. Dappling light over the rippled water was enough to navigate by. A mild southerly blew hair across his face when he yanked the cord to spark the outboard motor. He tried a few times to no avail, pulled the choke out a tad, and tried again. Mike then shook the petrol container and pumped the hose. *Bloody Henry, never fills the tank.*

Mike nearly fell overboard when he stumbled out of the small craft and staggered to the boat shed to retrieve the extra can of petrol and a funnel. He sat next to the boat filling the tank with shaking hands, swearing to himself, and pleading out loud, 'Wait for me. Cassie, I'm coming.'

Hearing the ruckus which his brother was making when he knocked things over in the boat shed, Henry sauntered down to help. Mike didn't see him coming until he heard the voice.

'Need a hand, mate?' Henry called, flicking a glowing cigarette butt towards the river.

The butt fell short of the river. A flash lit the sky when petrol fumes exploded. Flames sped along the spills Mike had created when trying in his drunken state to pour the fuel from the can through the funnel.

Henry immediately grasped the gravity of the situation when Mike's hair singed into flame. He threw his brother in the river to douse the fire. Mike screamed with pain, his eyes hot and stinging. Henry tried to wash them out and simultaneously yell to his parents to ring an ambulance.

Henry never told anyone, including Mike, that he was the one who'd thrown the butt which accidentally set the fumes ablaze from the petrol can. He was only trying to help Mike who, in his tipsy state, was spilling fuel everywhere. Henry blamed himself but didn't tell Mike, believing that, while he loved his brother, it would only cause bad blood between them. Henry made a decision that night to keep his secret to himself.

Nevertheless, over time, Henry felt compelled to offload his guilt.

One day with Anna, he broke down and told her the truth of his involvement, swearing her to secrecy. He also asked her to conceal Mike's blindness, until Mike had his own chance to tell Cassie his version of what had happened. Anna agreed. It was up to Mike to break his own news to Cassie, yet she didn't know how long she could hold her tongue, knowing Cassie was desperately waiting to hear from him.

By mid-morning when the excitement of the exam results had settled, and the boys had gone home, Anna rang Cassie. They chatted about which courses they would be enrolling in and Anna filled Cassie in on Mike's results. Before Cassie could reply, Anna quickly added that Mike had asked her to relay his results, because he and Henry had a full day helping their dad do an urgent job, hence he couldn't call her personally today.

A little deflated, Cassie ventured, 'Actually, Anna, Mum said I could get the train down the day after tomorrow, so I'll finally get to speak to him then, if not before…in fact, I might even surprise him and visit. What do you think?'

Anna's pause was only two seconds, but enough to alert Cassie.

'Well, do you think I should surprise him?'

Anna swiftly recovered into her bubbly self. 'I can't wait to see you and come straight to my place, and we'll work out a plan to surprise him.'

'Sounds good. See you soon,' Cassie said and hung up.

Anna now had extra time to sort out something before her friend arrived. Best to talk to Henry and wait until after Mike's eye appointment, just in case things had changed for the better…or worse.

Not long after lunch, Mike, his mum and brother Henry were sitting in the doctor's waiting room awaiting his eye review. Mike had been there a few times before and nothing had changed. He could still hear the gurgle of the fish tank aerator in the corner but couldn't see the silvery-bright little fish darting around, which his mother chatted about each time they were there. Feeling hopeful, Mike imagined that one day he might even see them.

'Come on in,' the doctor greeted the trio.

Mike's eye patches were removed.

The doctor peered each way with his magnifier headset on. He pulled a little at some contracting scar tissue at the edge of the right eye socket, then checked the left again, before flashing his light into the pupils to elicit if there was any reaction. After some eye drops and meaningless umming sounds, the doctor announced. 'Good news.' The doctor kept looking, and he ummed again. He hesitated. 'Well, actually, some good news and some bad news.'

Henry spoke. 'Well, doc, what's the good news?'

Mike sat quietly and his mother patted his hand.

The doctor smiled at her patience. 'I think the left eye has a good chance of further recovery. Don't get too excited. It will take a while but will regain sight, a little blurry at first, then reacting to light and you'll see shadows and outlines…but the bad news is the right eye seems to have suffered more of the burn, and I'm pretty sure you'll only get a little further recovery there. You never know, though, when things progress, we're always coming up with new research and ideas. Worst case scenario is you may end up with a right-sided glass eye, better than having a patch over it for the rest of your life, though.'

'That's wonderful, Mike,' his mother said, squeezing his hand, pretending she was looking forward to greeting her son with one fake eye.

Mike, forever the sceptic, asked, 'Doc, how long do you think my left eye will take to begin to regain some sight?'

'Can't say, perhaps another month, maybe a tad earlier, but you still need to patch it, to allow full recovery.'

The next day, as early as he could, Mike phoned Cassie. Enlivened, he felt her warmth through the phone line. It seemed like nothing had changed between them. He knew, however, his life had changed forever, and he wasn't going to burden himself on Cassie. Hence, he began the conversation by giving her a way out.

Without mentioning his blindness,Mike said, 'I've changed, Cassie.'

'We all have, Mike. I've grown up a lot this summer. I'm looking forward to starting teacher's college. What about you? Will you do engineering at UNSW or Sydney Uni?'

Mike paused. 'Not sure yet what I'll do. I've changed heaps. Maybe you don't want to hang around with me any more…'

'Don't be silly. I can't wait to see you. I've been waiting so long my heart is aching.'

Mike almost told her the truth but held back. 'I really would love to SEE you…' He wondered if he would ever see her round face, sparkling eyes, and silky flaxen hair again.

'Great, I'll be down tomorrow, and we can talk about things then. Gotta' go now, Mum's calling.'

The following day, after Cassie had arrived at Anna's, they caught up on as much goss as they could fit in before they met with Henry. Together, they strolled to the village plaza for pizza.

Once the girls had each had enough pizza, they left Henry to finish off the last four slices of pepperoni while they went for a walk. It was time for Anna to hatch the plan she'd related to Cassie earlier, to surprise Mike. Anna didn't want Mike to know they were coming. She also wanted to see the look on Cassie's face when she viewed Mike's patched eyes and dark glasses, while he worked out the flavours at the gelato bar. It would be a surprise for both of them. The girls had known each other's secrets for years. They could read each other to a tee. What Anna really wanted to know, though, was whether Cassie still loved Mike, enough to stay with him, but not out of pity.

'Don't say a word, Cass, I just want to you see Mike first, so let me do the talking,' Anna said.

'Why? What's going on?'

'He's messed up and doesn't know how to break the news to you…'

'What fuckin' news. I really want to see him.'

'Trust me on this one, Cass. Stick with me.'

'Hi, Mike,' Anna called, approaching Mike's workplace. 'We were just having a pizza with Hen and thought we'd grab a gelato. How's it going?'

'OK, quiet night. Thank god I'm not being heckled...yet.'

'I'll have a single vanilla cone and I'll take a cup of rum and raisin back to Henry.'

Cassie, who'd been sworn to silence, stared. A hidden well of pity temporarily swamped her. She attempted to say something, when Anna shushed her.

Anna then spoke. 'I've got a friend with me.'

'What can I get you?' Mike asked.

The catch in Cassie's voice was louder than any words she could speak. In a whisper, Cassie said. 'I'll have choc-chip please.'

Mike's face grew hotter. He wasn't quite sure if he'd heard right, but he recognised the voice. Feigning composure while his legs trembled behind the counter, he replied, 'Sorry we don't have choc-chip, just chocolate ripple.'

'Sounds perfect,' Cassie smiled.

Mike could not see her joy but, feeling her warmth, he smiled back. 'Is that my Cassie?'

'It's me and I'm back for good. When do you finish your shift?'

'Half hour or so, depends on the crowd.'

'I'm not going anywhere. I'll wait and have my choc ripple when you close.'

Later, the four friends walked home, Cassie and Anna in front and the boys lagging a fair way behind, Henry's arm linked through Mike's, while he steered him over the gutters and bumps.

'I'm so happy, Henry. Didn't think she'd accept me. So far, she seems okay about my eyes. I've never stopped loving her...and thank god I've got you, bro...'

Tears stung Henry's eyes. He wasn't sure if they were tears of joy for his younger brother reunited with Cassie, or tears of guilt. 'Mike, I've got to tell you something... You know the night of the accident?'

'Yeah, mate, we won't talk about it any more. I'm going to be okay. I've got Cassie, and you.'

'I need to tell you. It was me who flicked the lit cigarette butt which ignited the flames. I'm sorry.' Henry stopped, waiting to see his brother's reaction, fully cognizant Mike would possibly stumble if he swung a fist and tried hit him.

Instead, Mike grinned. 'I know, mate. I've thought about it lots. Even though I was drunk, I still know how to start a petrol motor without creating a spark. It was an accident, so don't beat yourself up about it.'

'Thanks,' Henry said, feeling the weight had finally been lifted from him for telling the truth. He then asked. 'So...you'll still be my best man at the wedding?'

Mike beamed. 'Only if you'll be my best man one day.'

Muffin Mistake?

Hettie Baker's fingers dangled from her wrist like a dead five-legged spider. Her muscles were floppy now and her strength dwindled, yet she appreciated at her age it would not be a sheer force which could kill her husband. Hettie sighed, knowing she would need to turn her mind to something simple and inane, whereby no one would ever suspect her, least of all George. Hettie would ensure she was seen to be the loving self-sacrificing wife to the bitter – yes, it was bitter – end.

The constancy of the cerulean skies over Sydney during summer began to nettle Hettie's frayed nerves. Due to daylight saving, the sunshine lingered well into an elongated evening. Hettie longed to go to bed. Nevertheless, the nights were fitful and fragmented when sleep eluded her more frequently these days. Perhaps it was because she still hadn't made the regular trip to the supermarket to secure the banana muffins which her dementing husband George requested every half hour or so. The delay in making a decision seemed all encompassing.

Tomorrow, Hettie said to herself, dragging one slipper off and then the other. She tucked herself into bed next to snoring George. She pushed him onto his side in one fell swoop, which nearly landed him out of the other side of the double bed. I should have taken the queen bed the kids offered, was Hettie's last thought as she drifted off.

Awaking to another endless day of sunshine, Hettie promised George today was the day. Yes, she would finally buy a six-pack of large muffins. Whispering under her breath as George smiled at his wife endearingly, she mumbled, 'Hope you bloody well choke on them.'

Once George's ablution needs were attended to, Hettie clacked his upper and lower dentures in place and plonked him in a chair. Then she covered him with a multicoloured crocheted rug she'd made years ago. Finally, Hettie poured him a cup of tea and cut up a crumpet with Vegemite – another of his favourites.

'Now, don't splosh your tea, George dear. I've only filled it halfway and I'll get you another before I go.'

Slow as an old reptile when it came to move himself about, George had a keen eye for a good cuppa. 'Low tide,' he muttered.

Hettie heard the chide. 'Yes, low tide. It's all the tea you get until I refill the cup, otherwise you'll spill it!'

Hettie hobbled off with the same thought hovering in her mind which had sat with her for the past few years, maybe even longer. She had a yearning for freedom and now, in her late eighties, longed for a few years, maybe not even that, for a little peace and quiet. Such a modest, yet seemingly unattainable goal.

Dressed in her street clothes and her Velcro-strapped comfy shoes, Hettie's quick glance in the mirror was enough to make her apply a single swipe of pink lippy across her creased mouth. The reflection of her bush-turkey neck swayed when she moved her head, prompting Hettie to throw on a scarf. She could no longer see to pluck the odd whisker on her chin, yet the ability to still feel them with her fingertips was a constant annoyance, knowing they were there and unreachable with her shaky hands. Oh yes, the hands. Hettie remembered those goanna-like claws needed softening. She squeezed a blob of sorbolene and rubbed thoroughly. With a flick of the brush through her grey wispy hair, Hettie was ready for the journey.

A short outing wasn't so easy these days. Hettie grabbed her purse, the car keys and her reusable – now mandatory – shopping bag. Gone were the days, she mused, when customers were greeted with plastic bags at every opportunity. There was no way she was going to pay the fifteen cents nowadays at the local supermarket. She silently berated the younger generation for using up the world's resources at such an alarming rate. She knew she and George rarely switched on lights and never used the air conditioner, unless the temperature rose to forty degrees Celsius, and their heater was used sparingly. What was wrong with putting on an extra pair of socks or a woolly cardigan and gloves on a chilly day? Yes, those young ones could easily learn a trick or two about sparsity from her older generation. Hettie would never throw out food scraps, everything was eaten, and if the vegies were a little limp, they would be slipped into soup or a stew.

The act of releasing and lifting her four-wheel walker from the boot seemed to get harder each day. The stupid contraption nearly got away from Hettie when the wheels inched over the boot rim before she could catch it. Of course, if George had seen the walker hit the car's paint, he'd have something to say. 'Well, George,' she said to his absence, 'I don't care if the bloody car gets scratched. You'll never see it anyway.'

Pushing the metal frame into the shop, Hettie grabbed the usual items, before eventually locating on a new shelf the muffins George craved. 'Done,' she said. At the checkout, she noticed a particularly nice bunch of white lisianthus. With a premature thought that perhaps they might be needed to mark an upcoming occasion, she purchased the flowers, knowing they would last well in a vase.

Once back in the thirty-year-old Corolla, Hettie stuck the key in the ignition and revved it to life. She reversed and slammed on the brakes when she banged into a walking frame from a neighbouring car – in another disabled spot. She called out her window, 'Keep within your lines. It's why they give silly old buggers like us wider spaces.'

With no time to hear a retort, Hettie zoomed away from the car park and down the back road to home, ensuring she kept clear of the young ones speeding in SUVs cutting in and out on the highway. Hettie constantly asked her extended family why they needed such big cars to clog the roads, only to be told the kids' car seats and baby carriers needed more space. 'Well, the babies and kids are no bigger than they always were,' she'd bark back, while met with an eye roll from her eldest granddaughter.

Home at last, Hettie swerved into her driveway, scarcely missing the neighbour's wheelie bin left on the road. Just one more thing to irritate her and mess up her day. Hettie hankered to tell the neighbour the council required bins to be taken in after twenty-four hours. Taking a deep breath, she sighed and thought better off it. Last time she swore at them about something, she found a dead possum near her front gate. It could have fallen out of a tree in the recent big storm, George said. However, Hettie was convinced the neighbours were up to no good.

Hettie arrived home to find George had newly woken from one of his many daytime naps.

'Will I, or won't I?' Hettie debated with herself, then called out to George. 'I'm home. I'll get you a cuppa. Do you want your muffins heated up?'

'Yes, thanks, luv,' croaked a voice from afar.

Why not, she thought. Hettie placed one and a half muffins into the microwave on high heat while she prepared the tea.

'There you go, George, nice and warm. Let them cool a little first.' She dabbed leaking dribble from his mouth, before warning him not to drink the tea, as it was very hot. 'Leave it until you've finished the muffin. I'm going outside to do a spot of gardening while the weather's fine. I need to water a couple of trees down the back, because I have to use a hand-held hose due to the watering restrictions. Pity you didn't get the watering system connected when I asked years ago.'

Hettie sighed. 'So don't try calling me. I won't hear you. Just enjoy those muffins, fresh today, the shop assistant told me.' Wiping another flood of drool from her husband's chin, Hettie hesitated, wondering if she should leave a glass of water to slake George's incessant thirst, but then walked away. 'Bye bye, George.'

An hour later, after she'd worked off some of her misery, Hettie imagined her future might still hold a small quotient of joy. She returned to the house to find George laying slumped in his favourite chair, which was nothing unusual, except his head hung to one side and his cloudy sea-glass eyes were stuck open and fixed. Quiet. Still.

Crumbs of dried muffin were scattered like birdseed over the floor and one of her bone china plates had cracked when it was dropped.

Dead. Finally. Hettie gave George a slight peck on his cheek. She whispered to his somewhat cool, lifeless body, 'It's been a long sixty years and I'm glad it's over. Had to happen sooner or later.'

Hettie then rang the doctor's surgery to let them know her husband didn't need his afternoon home visit because she had just found George dead in his chair.

'Mrs Baker, Hettie, you must ring the ambulance and I'll let the doctor know to meet you at your house. Cause of death and all that. I'm so sorry for your loss. It must be very hard for you. Can you get one of your daughters over to help?'

'No thanks, I'm okay by myself and I'm sure they will all come running when the word's out.' Hettie put the receiver back on the phone and began picking up pieces of the broken plate, cursing herself for having not given him one of the garish coloured plastic plates she reserved for the grandkids.

It wasn't long before the hordes arrived. The ambos skilfully shoved a laryngoscope with a tiny light down George's throat, only to discover a big hard crumbly mass at the back. It was impossible to pull out and once dislodged it retreated further down his airway.

The doctor was wise in his approach to Hettie. He had expected a heart attack at first until told about the obstructed trachea. Noticing the mess on the floor and after talking to Hettie, the doctor discerned it was the muffin which asphyxiated old George. Having seen cases like this before, he felt best to stay quiet on this one. Hettie, he imagined, was upset enough after dedicating her life to George's needs and demands.

'It's no one's fault, Hettie. Just one of those things. You have done a good job caring for him for so long.'

Hettie summed forthwith a few piteous tears to please the doctor, who patted her shoulder and spoke. 'Very sad for you, Hettie. We'll get your daughters to come over to be with you. Ring the surgery if there's anything we can do. George died from choking and a respiratory arrest. Pretty straightforward, so no need for a coroner's opinion in this case.'

Following the funeral service, the family gathered back at the house for tea and cakes.

Hettie's daughter spoke. 'Mum, you seem to be coping well. Good to see lots of mourners and Dad's old friends here. Even old Flo from next door turned up, which was nice.'

Hettie nodded while she arranged the finger sandwiches and heated a batch of mini-muffins in the microwave.

Ding, went the microwave, and ping went the sharp thought in her daughter's mind.

'Mum, remember I mentioned to you those couple of cases I read about in the *Health and Wellbeing* magazine…'

'About what?' Hettie feigned ignorance about how microwaving some foods changed the consistency once they started to cool…such as muffins.

'The texture hardens, Mum, making swallowing difficult,' her daughter said.

'Really?'

'Yes, Mum. Did you microwave Dad's muffin?' Her daughter spoke accusingly.

'He liked them warm, so I just turned on the…oven.'

Now alone, Hettie tentatively looked forward to the few good years she might have left. It was now her time to do what she wanted. Yet somehow all she seemed to do was look backward, into the past. Reflecting on the best times and bad times, Hettie tried to make sense of her life. Every so often, she pulled herself back to the present. She even toyed with the idea of reconnecting with a previous old beau, who she knew had been recently widowed. Maybe we could get together for a last hurrah. It could work out – even if only for a couple of years. And if not, Hettie pondered, there are always those new raspberry and white chocolate muffins at Woolies.

Sisterly Betrayal

Gabrielle and Gwendolyn were twins. As young girls, they would get up to the usual twin mischief, pretending to be each other and giggling when they exposed their pranks. Their parents could spot minor differences in their daughters' looks and temperament and often shouted out to scold them. Hence, it was at a young age they were called by derivatives of their names Gaby and Gwen. Once the girls were old enough, they moved out, flatted together and pursued lives of travel, study and work. It was Gaby, though, who always wanted to settle down and have children while Gwen was content to remain free and travel the world.

Gaby, however, was determined to follow her dream. She felt a slight shudder singe through her body when she walked towards the Picasso print at the end of her parents' hallway. The picture gave her the creeps. Thankfully, this would be the last night she would sleep in her childhood home. Tomorrow would be her wedding day.

The twins' father had worked for years packing and sorting in the backroom of the New South Wales Art Gallery. He had no formal or informal training for that matter in art history or appreciation. Nevertheless, he was in good company with his colleagues employed behind the scenes in the myriad of tasks the gallery required. They all knew what they liked and didn't like. Unable to afford expensive artwork, he often leafed through books, attended exhibitions and rummaged around the many unhung paintings awaiting their turn on the whitewashed walls upstairs. When his wife was pregnant with twins, he purchased a 1932 Picasso print of Marie Therese Walter, who was believed to be one of Picasso's many mistresses. The painting depicted the distinctive cubist period where the young woman exuded fecundity and sensuality as she observed herself in the looking glass.

Gaby and Gwen often made fun of the painting during their childhood. They giggled and mimicked the woman's expression and assigned the day and night versions of the painted face to each of themselves – depending on their moods.

As she grew up, Gaby found the print increasingly disturbing as she attempted to understand the facial expressions. Oftentimes, though, she felt serene when she finger-traced the colourful flowing lines which made up the whole of the girl. However, more recently, the dark lines seemed to develop an unusual edge as the hybrid Janus-faced girl with the swirling belly and rounded breasts stared mockingly back at her.

Following an unsettled sleep in her parents' home, Gaby awoke to the usual mayhem on her wedding day. Her mum was organising the hairdresser, make-up beautician, dress fitter, flower delivery and giggly bridesmaids, all there to assist her daughter to look beautiful for the lunchtime ceremony. The only person not present to fuss about her was Gwen.

The morning raced by, and the wedding time drew near, Gaby mused on past wrongs. She sneered, looked skyward to heaven and mouthed to her dead twin, 'There's no way you can have him now.' The memory of the night six months ago in the flat the sister's shared set off sparks of fury in Gaby. She overheard hushed tones through her sister's flimsy fibro wall and knew Gwen was speaking on the phone to Sebastian, the man Gaby was set to marry.

Eager to hear more of the conversation, Gaby crept from her bedroom to the bathroom adjoining her sister's room. She cupped her ear to the wall, close to where she knew Gwen would be lying with phone in hand. In doing so, she sat and leaned from the toilet seat when she glanced downward and noticed something poking out from under a bunch of fresh tissues in the bin, It was a tiny length of plastic. Gaby retrieved the pregnancy test stick, which revealed two distinctive blue lines. Muffling her rage, she returned to her room, seething. In that moment of rage, she hatched a plan to get Gwen out of her life forever.

*

Now, six months later, half a year had passed and her plan had worked. She was about to be married. Gaby stared in the mirror and screamed noiselessly, asking herself, 'So why, do I still see her?' Taking deep breaths to calm herself, Gaby continued to gaze at her own reflection as she sat quietly when her hair was pulled and twirled and shades of lipstick smudged on and off. She could hardly bear to see the face in the mirror, and eventually turned away. The only image she'd seen reflected towards her was of her now dead sister, mouth open gasping, falling backward off the sea cliff headland, eventually smashing onto the rocks below.

At the time of her sister's death, a fishing boat had swooped up Gwen's mangled body after she'd been tumbled and dragged in and out with the waves. Gaby immediately phoned her dad and the rescuers notified police and ambulance, who arrived at the scene and questioned anyone who witnessed the tragedy. Gaby said she'd been the only one there when Gwen fell and believed it was an accident. She told the police her fiancé Sebastian and a friend of his were a fair way behind, getting a barbecue started for their picnic. Sobbing, Gaby had related how her sister Gwen stumbled on loose stones and yelled for help, which was to no avail as she slipped down quickly. Nevertheless, the sergeant on the case didn't seem convinced, and the look on his face didn't go unnoticed by her father.

Fearing the loss of another daughter, Gaby's father reassured her. His voice choked on the words. 'No one's blaming you, sweetie. Gwen just stepped backward a little too far…she was always a daredevil.' Her father then turned his face away from his daughter.

Gaby knew his explanation wasn't quite true yet went along with her dad's version. She reiterated being the last person to see her sister alive – or so she had thought. However, she was also the one who urged Gwen closer to the edge to get the panoramic backdrop for the photos, which she snapped with her iPhone. She wondered later whether Sebastian had seen the incident but decided not to ask.

Afterwards police, suspected and questioned Gaby's fiancé Sebastian, who had arrived surprisingly soon after the incident, having left his best mate Joe scouting in the vicinity collecting wood for the barbecue they intended to have burning when the others returned.

It was Sebastian who had later suggested to Gaby to delay their wedding out of respect for Gwen. He was struck by the coldness of the volley of abuse from his fiancé, who seemed overly anxious to stick to the plan for the wedding to take place less than six months after her twin sister Gwen's death. Gaby offered no reason for this, preferring, even insisting, the date remained unchanged. There was no way she was giving up her wedding day for a sister who'd betrayed her in the worst possible way – and Sebastian could bloody well pay the price for his infidelity, she told herself.

*

Gaby sighed, bringing herself back to the present moment of her wedding day preparations, when her two twittering bridesmaids interrupted. 'Stop fiddling with your hair. Time to go.'

Sweeping up the train of Gaby's silk dress, her mum hugged her. 'You look gorgeous, darling. I only wish Gwen were here to see you...'

'Enough, Mum! I can't cope with that right now.'

Dabbing her eyes, her mother squeezed Gaby's hand and passed her over to her father before slipping out with the bridesmaids to their waiting car.

Holding his daughter firmly by the elbow to prevent her tripping when she wobbled in her stilettoes, he kissed her hand. 'You know, Gaby, it's not too late to pull out now if you want to.'

'Oh Dad, don't you see? I MUST marry Seb. He's mine now. The police still think he had something to do with Gwen's death and I need to show the world I love him.'

Her father sighed and shook his head as if he was ridding himself of a nagging guilt, unable to voice what he really felt happened. He still suspected Gaby of some foul play, aware of past rages his girls encountered with each other, yet he dreaded losing his remaining daughter. Looking forward, he stood tall and took one slow step after another and led his daughter to the white-ribboned Rolls Royce waiting to drive them to the church.

Crystal Clear

Pitter-patter, splat. Snug in my sleeping bag, I woke to a dull drizzly day. I couldn't see the point in getting up. It was a quagmire outside. Splat, splat, drip. The seams of the tent were now drenched and water seeped in. I eyed though the gauze opening and saw some campers slosh to the dunny block in rain jackets and muddy thongs. I closed my eyes once more. However, my bursting bladder kept me awake.

Rolling over the other way, I looked towards Main Beach, where the waves were small, flattened by the rain. Hang on – I rubbed my eyes. I couldn't even see waves yesterday from my sleeping bag. Where was Mum and Simon's tent?

I ripped down the zip down and wriggled out. Their tent was gone. No car, no them, no nothing. All cleared out, as if they'd never been there. Weird. Maybe my parents were going home early and couldn't find me at the pub to let me know. I scratched my itchy scalp; my hair was full of salt and knotted. Their bigger tent was next to my small one when I dossed down around midnight. I'd slid into my tent quietly hoping not to wake Mum. Simon was flaked out, as usual.

I needed to pee. With a foggy head, I dragged my body to the ladies' end of the toilet block. Usually I'd get dressed, but I was in a hurry so I threw a sweater over my pyjamas. I wanted to avoid running into the guys I met last night. Narrowly I missed a human rope of little kids clutching each other's hands. Their mother scolded them. 'Hang on, hurry up.'

Inside the toilet block, a queasy feeling overcame me when the stench wafted from the overnight build up, which was never cleaned until lunchtime. Pulling up my pyjama pants, I splashed my face at the basin and gave myself a fright when I glanced in the mirror. My bloodshot blue eyes had taken on a purplish tinge and the surrounding skin was pale, a bit like nocturnal animal caught in the headlights, maybe a numbat. Never fall asleep on the beach with sunglasses on, I told myself. And never ever go one for one, downing shots with Sandy!

I dawdled outside into the mud and nearly slipped when one thong became stuck. Over the way, the cute guy from last night with the blond dreadlocks headed towards the toilet block. I raised my hand to wave, but he'd already dived through the door. Another lost opportunity. He probably had a girlfriend anyway. I could see my lonely tent, now sunken in the middle, pooling with rainwater. I pondered what to do next as I ran my open fingers through my matted hair, breaking a few knots in the process.

'Hey, luvvy, you okay? You look like a lost puppy.' It was old Wal, the campground bloke coming to empty the bins.

'Yeah. Think so…I'm not lost…maybe my mum is?'

'Is that your tent over there?' He pointed east, and I nodded. 'I saw your parents drive off at sparrows' fart.'

'Where to? Did they say anything?'

'Your mum paid the camp fees and your tent hire, while your dad yelled from the car for her to get a move on.'

'He's not my dad, just her latest.'

'She was a bit flustered but did ask for an envelope and wrote a quick note.'

'A note?' I parroted. 'That's all!'

'Sorry, kid. Barb is in the office, she'll find it for you.'

Wandering towards the office, I tried not to look hurried – tried to conceal the fear churning in my gut.

Barb handed me the envelope. 'Sit over there out of the rain if you like.'

'Thanks, but maybe I'll take a walk to the weather shed.'

I bypassed the shed. It was full of little kids squealing and kicking balls.

Reaching the beach, I sheltered under a clump of trees. When the rain abated, my shaky hands opened the soggy letter. Fifty bucks fell out. For me, that was bad news. A thin leather bracelet with a single fake crystal was lodged in the corner of the envelope – a talisman like the ones Mum made for good luck.

The note was short and written in Mum's distinctive untidy scrawl.

Janury 1988

Angel,

Sorry had to go. Big truble coming. Simon said he'd tell cops. I could end up in jail.

Don't want you caught up in it. Go home to Grandma's house. We'll get our stuff and shut the house up. Rent not paid. Will leave your things next door with Jill.

I'll ring sometime. Not back for long wile. Don't try to find me. Love mum x

PS. finish school

I wished Mum had learnt to spell correctly; she always nagged me about doing my homework and getting the words right. Folding the note, I seethed. This was supposed to be our big holiday together as a family before I did my final Year 12 exams and before going off with friends to schoolies week. 'What the hell now, Mum?'

My eyes stung when I pulled off my T-shirt and dived headlong into the surf. 'Don't try and find me.' What did she think I was – six years old! 'I'll be eighteen at the end of this year, Mum,' I shouted into the wave. I recollected my stepfather Simon's words: 'Toughen up, kid'. This set me raging again. Prick. What would he know about my life? A full hour passed before my mind cleared.

The sun finally knifed through the clouds. I waited a tad longer while my gear dried out. Thinking about Mum, I tried to make sense of the situation. She'd left before for a couple of months – said she had to lie low. Another time, she slipped into hiding for a year with her new boyfriend – said she needed to start over. It didn't work out. Apparently, the boyfriend died suddenly under suspicious circumstances while with

Mum, although no charges were laid. In the end, his death was deemed an accidental overdose. Mum never revealed the full story, and I was too scared to ask in case she bolted again.

Thank God for Granny. I often sobbed in my bed when I was little. Gran would hug me while she made excuses for Mum. Growing up, I became used to my shifting home life, with a different father every few years. When each man left, I never saw them again. Simon had stayed around for five years since I was twelve. I guess I was in luck. Even though he was a slime bag, at least he helped me get my driver's licence. Mum couldn't teach me because she was usually zonked out when I arrived home from school.

Time to go now. I stood and stretched. The train to Sydney left in a couple of hours, which gave me time to pack up and walk to the station at Byron Bay.

The station was crowded with backpacks, boards and people coming and going on buses, to link with the train. The Rails Hotel was buzzing even though it was only mid-afternoon. I grabbed an OJ and a packet of crinkle-cut chips.

My girlfriend Sandy walked past. 'Where're you off to? I thought we were catching up for carrot cake at Twisted Sister café.'

'Home to see Gran. She's sick,' I half lied.

'Where're your parents? Their tent was gone when I came looking for you.'

'They had to go early to see Gran.' I fibbed again.

Sandy persisted. 'Why not get the next train and we can catch up with the guys before you go?'

'I'd better get going.' I faked indifference, though my heart and other parts of me were now alive, recalling Jake's soft touch the night before.

The train rattled into the station.

Sandy waved, 'Next time, eh.'

The train going south was packed full of travellers heading back for the beginning of the latter half of the school year. They were mostly young and didn't seem to care they'd blocked the aisles with their back-packs and assorted paraphernalia. I tripped over someone's guitar, which was standing upright against a seat. It fell face down onto the floor.

'What the fuck! Watch where you're going.'

'Sorreee…'

Jostling towards the end of the carriage, I spotted a vacant double seat and stuffed the rest of my gear onto the spare seat. Settled with a breeze through the window, I opened the chips and crunched my way through the entire pack. All gone. I licked my fingers and slurped the orange juice.

The train was now rollicking through the rolling green hills of the hinterland where macadamia and avocado plantations were dotted among small wooden houses aglow with orangey sunset. Mesmerised, I settled into the gentle rock of the train. The light faded and soon it would be dark. I hoped to grab a few hours' sleep before we reached Sydney at sunup.

In the evening, groups of teenagers gathered in the front of the car-riage and handed around beers, shots and joints. The familiar smell of hash wafted through the air. It seemed like a party, but I wasn't invited.

I'd never felt so lonely in my whole life – a bit like the last sausage roll in the warming tray at the servo. Nobody wants it and eventually it gets chucked away.

My imagination then failed me. I could no longer see Mum's face or pictures of my past or future life. It was like being in limbo – stuck. Inside my pocket I felt around and fished out the crumpled paper. Re-reading the note brought Mum back to me. I wasn't so angry now, yet still bewildered about what her 'big problem' might be. I visualised the tilt of her head, her long chestnut hair and sparkling green eyes. I smelt her 4711 scent and wondered if I should save up and buy her a special perfume for her birthday, if and when she'd ever come back.

Mum was feisty at times. Still, underneath I sensed her vulnerability when she was lured from one disastrous relationship to another. I re-called her coming home each day, after washing up in the greasy diner kitchen and working behind the counter at the local servo. Oftentimes she'd bring home a few leftover rolls or pies for dinner. The manager liked her and tolerated her comings and goings. Even though she couldn't spell, it didn't matter. Mum was good with numbers and always tallied the till correctly. She'd never had a problem with cutting her stash of hash or cocaine, and always seemed to make a bit on the side when dealing drugs – 'for your school things,' she said. I reread the end of her brief note, 'PS. finish school.' I drifted off.

The train hissed into Hornsby station and a hint of early sunshine touched the window. I must have slept for at least eight hours and mercifully so did the partygoers up front. I unwound my curled-up body and grabbed my gear, shoved my way onto the platform, then through the turnstile. At the bus terminus, I found none were going my way for another hour. Luckily, a taxi was waiting at the rank. I splashed out with the remainder of the fifty bucks and went straight to Gran's. I wasn't up to going to our old neighbour's place first to pick up my stuff from Jill – because I couldn't cope with the nosy questions and her 'Tut-tut, poor girl' just yet.

The taxi pulled up outside the brick cottage in Waitara. As usual, Gran was sweeping her front veranda, keeping a lookout for my arrival. The skin at the edges of her eyes crinkled when a smile lit her face. She squeezed me. 'It'll be okay, Angel.'

'Mum's gone again.' My eyes misted.

'Come inside and eat first, then we'll talk.' Gran ushered me inside and straight through to the backyard. 'Now go and feed the birds while I make breakfast.'

Gran never sat down to a serious discussion on an empty stomach and she knew I'd be starving. She had also delayed the morning ritual of feeding her feathered friends in the aviary. It would keep me occupied while she cooked. The birds flocked and sang when I threw seed and grasses into the cage, before I checked and filled the water troughs. They were all small birds, protected from bigger hungrier ones squawking around the garden. A kaleidoscope of colour circled and chirped; lemon canaries, blue and green budgerigars, and a few tiny red-beaked finches with white and brown breasts.

Back inside, Gran served up crispy bacon and fried eggs with yolks still runny, so I could wipe my plate clean with toast. A schooner glass – one Mum had nicked from the pub – was full of icy milk. Gran didn't believe in bottled fruit juice, and always maintained the best juice to be had was sucked straight from the oranges and mandarins in her backyard.

When I'd finished eating, I told Gran the saga of how I'd woken in the campground to find Mum and Simon's tent gone. I couldn't believe they were in such a hurry they didn't wait to tell me what was going on, except for the words Mum had hurriedly scribbled and left at the office.

Gran was silent while I read Mum's note.

'Gone,' I said. 'No goodbyes? Must be something going on.' I lifted the paper with my thumb and forefinger and let it flutter to the floor.

Gran didn't bend to pick it up. Her eyes swept across my face, seeing the hurt behind my bravado. 'We'll sort things out somehow.'

An envelope addressed in Mum's handwriting to Gran, Thelma Kelly, sat on the kitchen bench. Gran opened it to show me Mum had sent her a note and a wad of money.

'What did she write to you, Gran?'

'Not much more. She wants me to look after you until she gets home, and there's no word of when that will be. She wants you to finish school, though, something I always wished she'd done for herself.'

'Where is she?'

'Don't know. She says she'll get in touch when she can.'

I tried to picture what Mum was doing now and where she might be, yet all I could think of was the note and why she hadn't waited to talk to me. Bloody Simon! How dare he threaten her with jail. Did I miss something?

'So, what next, Gran?'

My grandmother tried to disguise her world-weariness while she flapped around the kitchen. 'We wait. I know she'll come back.'

True. Mum always returned and each time tried her best to be motherly and provide me with her version of a normal life. She knew Gran was there to pick up the pieces and sort out her daughter's messes. An idea stuck me. I'd also seemed to be doing the same for Mum, since I was about ten.

Only a few days left of the mid-year break and then it would be headlong into my final year and Higher School Certificate. My days were full of lots to do catching up with Sandy and other friends. I also moved my stuff from the previous neighbour's house, timing it to dodge Jill, who was out at the time. Living at Gran's was comfortable, it was close to school, and she usually left me to my own devices, knowing we'd always catch up over dinner. I helped with chores in the garden and fed the tweeting birds while cleaning out their aviary.

Back at school, I liked the routine of assignments, assessments and then the trials. It gave structure to my life and defined the milestones of the year up until the exams, after which I intended to work more, buy a car, and drive up the coast on schoolies week, maybe even see Jake. I'm a bit of a dreamer; he probably wouldn't even remember me.

Night times were the worst. Trying to get to sleep was tough. I tossed and turned, wondering how much information slimy Simon had on Mum, and why he considered it enough to send her to jail. Ultimately, I relaxed. My body stilled when my mind settled on an image of Mum's face framed by her long hair. Compared with other mothers at the school, mine looked pretty good. She wasn't fat or frumpy. Mum had always been slim and resembled a much younger person in her flowery skirts, skimpy tops, dangly earrings and no make-up – a bit of a leftover hippie. Thank God, she didn't name me Rainbow or Sky.

A couple of years ago, some of the guys called her Mrs Robinson. I didn't know what they were talking about and queried it. 'Ask your mum,' they said.

Of course, once I asked Mum, I understood the reference to *The Graduate* movie, though I wasn't quite sure how to take it. I decided that, when compared to their mums, it might be a compliment. My mum was still pretty hot – for a mother. Then again, she's only thirty-three, so I can understand why she didn't want my friends to call her Mrs Kelly (she never married), and insisted they call her by her first name, which is Celeste. 'Just call me Star,' she'd say.

I smiled when I recalled her saying those words, and had almost fallen asleep, when another notion dawned on me. Mum never told me how old she was when I was born, but I knew her birthdate, and it didn't take long to figure it out. I'm seventeen now, a year older than when Mum must have had me, aged sixteen! I used to wonder how old my real dad was, or is. Mum was absolutely tight-lipped when I asked about him. She'd repeat her standard reply: 'When you're bigger, I'll tell you all about it.'

I jolted upright in bed. 'For God's sake, Mum, aren't I old enough now?'

Each day after school, I'd arrive home to find an empty letter box. It didn't stop me asking Gran if she'd heard from Mum.

'Not today, Angel…maybe soon.' Gran tried to be upbeat.

After food and chores, it was onto homework and study. I longed for the year to finish so I could head north on a road trip. All this kept my mind off craving for Mum's homecoming, tangled with constant wonder about what the hell was going on with her and Simon.

On weekends, Gran cooked up a big breakfast with scrambled eggs, bacon and tomatoes. We would sit a while longer perusing the paper for anything interesting…and checking the obituaries. Gran always pulled out the crossword page to do later when I wasn't around. She usually had it nearly finished before she'd let me tackle the few remaining words.

'Ah, can't believe I missed that one,' Gran would say when I captured the correct word for the clue.

'Anyway, what's this one? Germaine…?' I asked.

'Easy, it's Greer.'

Responding to my puzzled look, Gran explained she was a women's liberationist who wrote *The Female Eunuch* in 1970. 'The same year you were born. Lots of women bought the book. It opened our eyes to women's rights, inequality and why things needed to change.'

'Did Mum read it?'

'Bits here and there, but Celeste was still young – and pregnant. She ended up leaving halfway through third year of high school. You know your Mum did a brave thing having you. She never once contemplated otherwise, so your grandfather – bless his soul – and I supported her decision and helped out a lot when you were young.'

'Not much has changed, Gran.' I grinned and watched Gran's eyes sparkle before she continued.

'In those days, if it was too late to have an abortion, teenage pregnancy was still frowned upon. Girls were often sent away from their families to a home until they had the baby, which was usually adopted out. Sometimes, the mothers didn't even get to hold their bubs.'

'I guess I'm lucky she did.'

'What, hold you or have you?'

'Both, Gran. I miss her heaps. You know, she always said she'd tell me about it when I got older. She never did, though, and I've always wondered who my father is.'

'I guess it's a conversation you need to have with her. I never met your biological father and for some reason Celeste evaded my attempts to discover who he was. She didn't even let the hospital staff know his name, and it's not listed on your birth certificate. I do know, however, it wasn't anyone from school or around here. She told her best girlfriend at the time, but I think they lost touch years ago.'

'One day, I'll find out more.'

Gran stood to clear the plates. 'Go grab your netball gear, Angel. I'll drive you to the oval.'

A couple of months into the second half of the school year, it finally happened. I arrived home to a smiling Gran, who told me Mum had rung, to wish her a happy birthday. (Thanks for the reminder, Mum.)

'Oh yeah, happy birthday, Gran. I'll take you to the Chinese restaurant for dinner. What did Mum say?'

'She said happy birthday,' Gran chuckled.

'And?'

'She said she'd finally had enough of Simon and she's biding her time to get away from him. I expect things turned sour after he threatened her. Now she's devising a plan to come home.'

'When?'

'Don't know for sure. Apparently they're in the outback on a cattle station, doing a bit of camping and getting the odd jobs. Celeste does domestic work and Simon works on the trucks, fixing them and sometimes doing a long-haul cross-country. I think her plan is to take off when he's away for a few days.' Gran seemed preoccupied about something and fiddled with her apron as she gazed into the garden.

'Is she okay, Gran? Did she say anything about me?'

'Sorry, Angel. Just thinking. She's not okay by the sound of things. I could hear the quiver in her voice. She said to tell you she loves you more than anything and to do your best in the assessments, and she'd call one evening…if she can get use of the phone. In the end, the call was brief. She said bye for now, and hung up in a hurry.'

Months came and went. The HSC exams loomed. I was ready and couldn't wait for them to be over so I could get going and look for Mum. I had saved a bit from my part-time job, enough to buy a bomb car. I set about stashing it full of things I'd need, as I remembered them. The items included clothes, sleeping bag, a blanket, a towel, a fry pan and saucepan to go with the two-burner gas cooktop Gran gave me for birthday. I had seven exams to complete before I threw the last item in the car – the Esky full of ice, food, and bottle of champagne.

Everyone else in Year 12 seemed to be in a full panic mode when the first exam paper, English, was handed out. Easy for me, I was good at creating stories and could twist any topic into something interesting. I came home feeling elated, ready to tell Gran how it went.

A familiar whiff of 4711 perfume wafted down the hall when I entered the front door. Mum glided down the hall like a rosella in her rainbow flowing clothes.

'Hi, darling, I'm back.' She hugged me tight.

'Where've you been?' I asked when she unfolded her wings to release me.

'Up north on a station in the outback. It's a long story. How have *you* been and how did the exam go today? Thought I'd better be back while the exams were on to give you some moral support and spend time with you.'

Mum was buoyant, though a little jittery, with her hands flaying every which way. I was glad she was home, but her timing couldn't have been worse. I needed to focus on the rest of the exams before I could get involved with other things, especially Mum's complicated affairs.

'Great to see you, Mum. I'm pretty busy with study at the moment. How about we do stuff together after that?'

Gran called from the kitchen. 'Come down here, you two, the tea's brewed.'

I sat opposite Mum while I filled Gran in on my day and we morphed into our usual idle chitchat, while she cut into a slab of fruitcake.

Gran looked worried. Mum was silent.

'What's up?' I ventured to break the ice.

'Your mum's in a bit of a dilemma, Angel, and we need to try and sort it out. Maybe keep quiet for a bit and not tell anyone she's here.'

'Why?'

'Sorry to worry you, Angel, but Simon had a bit of misfortune at the cattle station,' Mum said in a matter-of-fact tone before adding, 'He's dead.'

'Dead! How?' A tinge of déjà vu nagged at me. Not that I liked the guy, but he did keep Mum out of trouble for a few years.

'It was in the kitchen where I did most of the cooking. Breakfast, lunch, dinner, plus cakes and snacks. All the pots and pans were so bloody heavy. Cast iron. You think I was cooking for a hundred, not twenty, by the size of the platters.'

'Get to the point, Celeste,' Gran said.

'Not sure if you knew, Angel, but Simon and I had been arguing a bit lately. He was going to dob me into the coppers for something I did years ago…nothing really for you to worry about.' Mum flicked her hand as if it was an isolated incident before continuing her story.

'It happened one morning when breakfast was finished and all the station hands were setting out for a roundup to bring the cattle in. They use motorbikes, dogs, horses, and sometimes helicopters to fetch them from miles around. Quite a sight when the cattle hoof up a dust storm and come tramping home to be corralled, ready for the big road trains to take them across the Barkly…'

'Mum, what happened?'

'He pissed me off when I was scraping the heavy baking dish, the one I frizzle three kilos of bacon in.'

Gran rolled her eyes and sighed.

'Anyway, it was full of bacon fat and he grabbed me around the waist. I think in hindsight it was maybe a bit of fun…but well, something in me snapped. I swung around so fast and somehow lifted the pan as high as I could and slammed it into his skull.'

'Did you mean to do it?' I was shaking my head in disbelief.

'Not sure. Perhaps it slipped. I was frazzled at the time and had heaps more washing up to do. Anyway, the long and short of it was, he slumped to the ground. Blood gushed from a big split in his head. His eyes looked like a three-day-old fish. It was at that point I realised he was dead. I panicked.'

'Then what? Did you call for help?'

'Lucky for me one of the guys was heading to town on a long drive for supplies so I cadged a lift with him. I told him Simon was still in the kitchen sorting out the washing up and getting lunch ready.'

'You lied! Why wouldn't you seek help, Mum…*if* it was an accident?'

'That's the point, Angel. I'm not sure it was an accident. I wanted him dead. In fact, I'd dreamed about it for a while. Just didn't think I'd be the one to do it.'

'So how did you get here?'

'I told the guy who gave me a lift I needed to get back to see my daughter, because she needed me to be around for her final exams.'

I kept tight-lipped as Gran gave me a wink.

Mum rattled on. 'I mentioned to the guy that Simon said he could manage on his own in the kitchen for a while. Once in town, I hitched a lift to the closest airport and caught the first plane out.'

'Great! Glad to have you back, Mum. However, this could possibly be a murder charge and you need to figure out what to do. Maybe you could tell the cops it was self-defence. Someone's going to smell a rat and they'll come looking for you.'

'Don't worry, Angel. Things will be okay now I'm back to look after you.'

'For Chrissake, Mum, it's not all right.'

I needed some fresh air, so I left the table and strode outside into the yard. I wanted to commune with someone sensible, so I talked to the chooks. Mum was as wacky as ever, though this time probably in real trouble. I didn't want to lose her again – she was all I had apart from Gran – yet I didn't know how we could live with this lie hanging over us.

After an hour, I meandered back to the house, where Mum and Gran were busily cooking. I needed more space, so left them in the kitchen and retreated to my room. 'Call me when dinner's ready. I need to study for tomorrow's second English paper.'

Two hours later, the banging on the front door startled me from re-vising old essay papers. I peeked out to view the visitors, and heard Gran desperately trying to explain that Mum was gone.

I ran to the door, where two uniformed police officers were attempting to enter and search the house while flashing a warrant. They said my mum was being charged for the murder of Simon Bradley.

'Maybe it was self-defence,' Gran pleaded.

'Not this time, Mrs Kelly. Unlike the last time, there was a reliable witness at the scene.'

Gran wailed as she approached me, arms outstretched to wrap me into her embrace, once again, 'She's not here and I don't know where she's gone. The last thing she said was, "Tell Angel I love her and to do your best in your exams."'

'She didn't even come to say goodbye!'

'She rocketed out in a hurry, Angel. We won't be seeing her for some time.'

Suddenly my mind cleared. I knew then it would be just Gran and me in the future and whatever happened we'd be there for each other. I still held onto my post-exam plan and couldn't wait to head off travelling. I would not be searching for Mum as I'd intended. I yearned to find myself instead.

The Funeral

World-weary, Ada sighed and said to herself, ' Just put one foot in front of the other.' She then recapped her mantra before while preparing for the day: 'Ada Featherstone, you should always dress nicely for a funeral.' She made sure her tailored black suit was pressed and clean before she touched it up with a discreetly coloured blouse. She ensured that her make-up was subtle, yet well applied with the obligatory waterproof mascara. Of course, her jewellery wouldn't be too gaudy or outlandish. The word for a funeral event came down to 'poised'.

Ada's lizard-like skin had dried and cracked like falling autumn leaves, once supple now frail. She applied some moisturiser to her shaky limbs, which had bent like aged branches gnarled at the joints.

Once satisfied she was ready, Ada held her head high in readiness for the funeral, which she envisaged would be no different from the many previously attended, except today she was farewelling someone she dearly loved. Ada predicted the mourning would be intensified with each eulogy, whereby people's emotions would pill forth real and heartfelt. Nevertheless, it could also be an opportune time to keep one eye out to see if any suspects lingered in the pews. She'd watched plenty of detective movies and always noticed after a crime scene, where death was the outcome, there was a policeman or two hovering in the background of the funeral scene, trying to elicit who might be a person of interest in the case.

Of the many funerals Ada had attended over the years, there was one which stuck in her head as she recalled the overt display of raw emotion. It took place in a Greek Orthodox church where a very much loved elderly woman, who had been terminally ill, lay in an open coffin. Lifeless, cold, serene. The congregation waited to view her body and say final goodbyes.

Her husband, a very old man, displayed his unmasked grief with such rawness that it bordered on being comic. He grabbed his wife and pulled her torso out of the coffin and kissed her while wailing, 'I love you, I love you, I can't leave you, Helena.'

This was much to the distress of his daughter, who grabbed her father, slapped him on the wrist and cried, 'Leave her alone, Dad, let her rest, put her back, put her back…'

This was probably not unusual for many European departures. However, to add to the scene, once the coffin was placed in the hearse at the completion of the ceremony, Helena's husband started wailing again. The coffin had to be reopened from the back of the car so he could pull his wife out once more – for a final kiss. The younger grandchildren, who hadn't witnessed such overt emotions, were quite astounded, and Ada saw a quick flash of text as one of them placed a note on Facebook, 'OMG…' et cetera.

Many funerals, though, are a relief for the family, especially if the person who's died was old or very debilitated. In the end, it was time to let them go.

Today's funeral differed, however. It was for the death of a young woman which took place under suspicious circumstances, possibly foul play. While the service would be woeful, Ada knew it would be overlaid with rage and remorse, leaving her with a gap which could never be filled. It was her godchild Bridie, and she was determined to find her killer.

Ada questioned her own ability to maintain composure. The anger she felt gnawed from deep within and she wanted to howl like an animal caught in a trap. A trap of grief from which she never imagined breaking free. Yet the one thing which kept her alive and focused was the need for revenge.

So Ada set off in her best black funeral suit and headed to the chapel. The small stone church wasn't far away, and the day was bright. She decided to stroll and look out at the same time. The first person she saw lurking in the church's tiny graveyard was a young man who looked like he'd just woken from sleeping under a tree. The matted hair at the back of his head resembled a regurgitated feline fur ball.

'Why can't the youth of today put a bit of an effort into their appearance?' she mumbled, before admonishing herself for uncharitable feelings towards the poor boy, who might have been homeless. Ada shivered involuntarily. He might even be a murderer.

It wasn't long before the churchyard and chapel filled with mourners. Ada nodded to those who came up to greet her while she dabbed her eyes to see each new face.

'Oh, Ada, so sad for you. She was a lovely girl. Those last few years took their toll, though.'

'She wasn't a girl,' Ada said. 'She was a young woman about to turn thirty-two.' Dab, dab.

Ada walked away to confront another familiar face. Her neighbour this time, Sam Carmody.

He whisked her away from the throng. 'How's it going, Ada? Let's catch up when this circus is over and have a few quiet wines together.'

Ada nodded and jigsawed her way through the gathering when one of the funeral directors approached her.

'Ms Featherstone, is there anything you'd like to say after the eulogies. I understand you were very close to Bridie. Just let me know.'

'I don't think so, but I'll call you if I change my mind,' Ada replied. She longed to escape the hordes, yet suddenly remembered the need to keep a close watch on everyone in attendance. She was certain whoever caused Bridie's death would be here to witness her burial.

Listening to the platitudes during the service, Ada's mind kept drifting back to the night Bridie died. How did it happen? It was an early spring blustery evening when a rain squall ripped across Sydney harbour. Usually, it was warming up at this time of year. However, on that night, it felt like winter had returned. Bridie had texted her godmother early on Friday morning to let her know she'd come and stay overnight on the Saturday, to see her for her sixty-first birthday. Such an attentive godchild, Ada recalled. Bridie always remembered the little things and became like a daughter to Ada ever since her mother had died when she was aged ten. Her father had remarried and now had a younger family. He moved interstate after Bridie had left home, so, fortuitously for Ada, it meant they could enjoy regular dinners and special occasions.

Still reflecting on Bridie's death, Ada rehashed in her mind the coroner's and police reports. It seemed Bridie went to work in the city as usual on the Manly ferry on the Friday morning. While at work' nothing seemed amiss. Bridie left her office about six thirty p.m. and changed into a simple black dress and stilettos, then touched up her make-up to go for drinks with friends at a city nightclub. Even though many of the revellers drank into the wee hours of the morning, Bridie was always content to get home for the weekend. This meant catching the last ferry to Manly wharf at eleven forty-five p.m., which would get in at twelve fifteen a.m. A brisk walk and she'd be home in bed within half an hour.

The wind had picked up to near gale force by the time Bridie tapped on her Opal card and alighted the ferry. She had donned her navy woollen coat and looped the waist belt, before wrapping a silk scarf around her neck to keep warm. Inside the ferry it was cosier, though still blustery when passengers walked in and out of the deck doors. Many young people, some friends of Bridie's included, shared last drinks on the ferry while it lurched from side to side crossing Sydney Heads. The giggly girls on the boat were raucous and Bridie felt a bit woozy from the wine and sea swell. She had rugged up and slipped outside onto the deck for some fresh air.

The reports showed, after the questioning of other passengers aboard, that a colleague, Angus, had followed Bridie out to check if she was okay. He said she had told him she felt fine and just needed some time out. Angus then retreated inside to escape the wind. When the ferry arrived at Manly wharf, there was the usual mad scramble to gather belongings and disembark, in the hope of catching the last taxi or bus home up to the northern beaches peninsula.

When asked if anyone had seen Bridie get off, Angus volunteered, 'Yes, she hurried off with others when it started to rain. I saw the back of her heading towards her place, which wasn't far away.'

It wasn't until three days later, when a woman's body was found washed up on rocks near the end of Quarantine Bay, that the police attempted to find out the identity and cause of death. The report noted they had previously received a phone call from Ms Ada Featherstone, who was concerned her godchild hadn't turned up to visit her as planned. The police noted her concerns and reassured her they'd follow up. They carried out their usual searching and questioning. One of the most obvious leads was to check all the Opal card tap-offs from the Friday night ferry journey. However, they were told, on those services, where there are no stops between the city and Manly wharf, tapping off the Opal card is not required. Even though Bridie's identity was confirmed, the authorities never found her phone, though Ada had alerted them that she still had the text messages Bridie regularly sent her. The coroner's conclusion was that Bridie died from 'Drowning by misadventure'. For Ada, many questions beckoned unanswered.

The funeral ended and 'Amazing Grace' played when the coffin was lifted by pallbearers. It jolted Ada out of her memories. She needed to focus on any clues, especially among the younger crowd Bridie had worked and associated with. The four young men carrying the coffin did so with reverence. Even the dishevelled fellow she'd seen wake earlier from sleeping under a tree assisted. Thankfully, he had tidied himself up a bit. Ada noticed tears drip down his cheek, which he couldn't wipe away lest the coffin toppled. He sniffed hard. Yet he seemed genuinely sad, if not a tad troubled by the situation, especially when his fellow pallbearer opposite gave him a fierce look which caused his face to redden. Once the coffin was placed in the hearse, the mourners headed for a cuppa and a drink, along with a light buffet lunch, to chat with each other before moving on.

Ada couldn't face the crowd, so headed away to sit on a cedar bench under a tree at the hedged periphery. No one missed her. She reflected how vexing it was that when women turned sixty, they tended to become invisible. The garden was peaceful, and she felt her grief wane as her jangled nerves settled. Ada closed her swollen eyes to quell a sting of salty tears.

From behind the hedge, Ada heard the voices of two young men, the pallbearers.

The dishevelled lad spoke to the pallbearer who had been opposite him, 'You bastard, Angus, how could you carry her coffin knowing what you did?'

Ada leaned in closer into the thicket of leaves to discern more. She knew the name Angus from texts and chats with Bridie. He had been harassing her at work. From what she told Ada, he never seemed to take no for an answer, while she tried to maintain nothing more than a friendship. Bridie even asked her godmother once if she'd thought he was stalking her. Ada remembered saying she needed to ask her higher executive boss to somehow deal with it, because Angus was her line manager. At the time, Bridie didn't want to upset things or create office gossip, so she let it go.

From behind the hedge a harsh whisper from Angus came next. 'Listen, Ben, it was an accident. She slipped on the wet deck in those bloody stilettos. I tried to rug her up, so I tied her flapping coat belt.'

'Liar,' Ben said in a louder voice. 'I saw you both struggle and you pulled her scarf so tight she gasped and slumped.'

'So we had a tiff, but I loved her. Then I went inside to go to the toilet. So that's my story,' Angus said.

Ben persisted. 'I don't believe you. It doesn't add up. We never saw Bridie on board after we crossed the Heads. You pushed her overboard!'

'Bullshit. I saw her get off and head home. I told the police.'

'You said you saw the back of her, yet all the girls were rugged in dark coats in the rain. It could have been anyone.'

'Listen, Ben, I didn't do it.'

'Well, explain to me, Angus, why did the coroner's report say her body had odd marks on her neck.'

'It was probably because her scarf got caught and tightened in the wind.'

Ada heard a rustle when Angus walked away towards the other mourners. Sensing Ben was still behind the hedge, she remained silent, until she heard him sob and speak softly to himself.

'Why would she double-knot her coat belt? I know you pushed her, Angus, and even if she wasn't dead when she hit the water, her coat would have been heavy enough to pull her down in the sea swell!'

Ada wobbled in the spongy grass and stood on her spindly legs in her heeled shoes, which she only wore on special occasions. Not wanting to scare Ben away, Ada walked slowly and attempted to kneel beside him. As it happened, she stumbled, and he grabbed her elbow to stop her fall. Ada told him she had been eavesdropping behind the hedge.

'Well, I suppose you heard all of it then,' he said. 'But no one will believe me. Angus seems to have watertight excuses.'

'I believe you, Ben, and I think we should talk with the police again.'

'They'd never listen to me… I've got a bit of a record for drugs and…'

'They will if we both go together. Whatever you did in the past doesn't have anything to do with Angus's actions. Anyway, I can tell you most women don't double-knot loose coat tie belts.' Ada grinned. 'They just require a quick loop. It's the quickest way to get it on and off, especially of you need to go to the toilet. I think we have enough clues for the police to at least re-look at the evidence.'

Ada patted Ben's hand and he nodded. She opened her mouth to reassure Ben when faces appeared from behind the bushes.

'Thought we'd find you here, Ben. We've been waiting,' the male police officer said.

Ben twitched, ready to bolt when the female office placed a firm hand on his arm. 'It's okay, we're not arresting you, but we did overhear some of your conversation and would appreciate you coming to the station to fill in some caps. I'm certain we can take a new look at the evidence and hopefully arrest the killer soon.'

'It was Angus,' Ben blurted.

'We've already taken him in for questioning,' the officer reassured.

'Thank heavens.' Ada's voice slipped out like a whispering breeze. Her smile filled the wrinkles in her cheeks and her eyes crinkled like scrunched cellophane.

Ada then held her emotions tight and strode erect with purpose towards home, so as not to appear a shattered old lady – knowing she would break down later, in her own private space, to mourn her beloved Bridie.

Unravelling

Madeline and Christophe grumbled along through winter. Madeline's emotions thawed with the snow in springtime when sunshine melted the ice. Creeks trickled at first then roared icy water over pebbles and rocks. Eventually, the slush on the hillside turned to grasses dotted with wildflowers. Madeline knew life had begun afresh – for a while at least.

Times were good for both Christophe and Madeline when they originally moved to the Snowy Mountains. They built their log cabin in a deep valley – even though the steep dirt road was barely accessible utilising a four-wheel drive. They were young, in love and very much the couple to know in the ski community. Christophe had emigrated from Austria after spending a few ski seasons in the hills – not mountains, as he was constantly at pains to point out – in the area around Thredbo in southern New South Wales. Madeline, a local girl, had worked in the ski fields each season for as long as she could remember. She knew every bend in the winding roads through the valleys which she traversed each year from her home in Canberra.

Madeline skied well and improved markedly under the close tuition of Christophe. Easily lured by his charm and good looks, she was soon in love. Christophe connected with Madeline's vitality when he watched her fling her sandy-haired ponytail with each ski run down the slopes.

At the end of his first season in the Snowy Mountains, Christophe asked Maddy to marry him. He took the liberty of organising a big wedding on the slopes with most of the regular ski community invited. On later reflection, Madeline wondered who all those people were who attended their very public ceremony. She huffed and realised only a few of them had bothered to stop and chat, or give her a call, since her terrifying tumble two years ago.

Well, she mused, it was more than just a tumble. A cavalcade of images flooded Madeline's mind. She remembered the day her skis flew out of control underneath her, leaving her dangling over a precipice. Those memories still sent her heart racing and her face flushing crimson with rage. It was not her fault!

Their friends believed Madeline's anger towards Christophe was misguided. They did not quite accept her story when she tried to explain his overly zealous nature, whereupon he'd pushed her well beyond her capability on a difficult black run. They always assumed Christophe was the 'good guy'. Hard on her heels one day, Christophe's skis clipped the back of Madeline's, causing her to skid off the side of a crevasse. Hanging over an ice ledge, her skis tangled, leaving her right leg twisted and broken in multiple places. A bone protruded though bloodied skin. Her leg was so badly damaged Maddy knew she'd never ski again. Once her body healed, she still found walking with the withered and callipered limb a chore.

Worse still, Madeline found herself confined to their log cabin the entire winter, because she couldn't drive the dangerous access road from their property. Christophe constantly reminded her it was far too tricky and slippery to negotiate with her car's disabled hand controls, and he didn't want her to have an accident. Madeline presumed at the time he was fussing unnecessarily, yet she was also pleased he cared so much. It was months before she fully realised that, during the miserable winter days of the snowbound months, Christophe would sneakily take her car keys with him whenever he ventured out. Mostly, he would join other skiers in afternoon jollity which, more often than not, continued long after sundown with schnapps and glühwein.

Occasionally, Madeline would be taken by her husband shopping at the nearby village on weekends, or perhaps to the pub on Saturday night at the Ski-tube station. Oftentimes, after one drink, she'd find herself sitting alone, while others hustled about chatted freely. Sometimes they gave her a wave or a smile. Christophe's poor disabled wife – she knew the look.

Madeline also knew the looks that Christophe received from those same people – the ski-bunnies – who pawed her husband, mesmerised by his stories of great runs down moguls and tricky passages through the snow gums. Every so often, Madeline sensed her heart was more brittle than her damaged leg.

The usual arguments followed on their drive home when Madeline accused Christophe of infidelity. 'What is it with you, Christophe? You can't stop swooning over those girls. How do you think it makes me feel sitting there alone?'

'But I want to take you out. You're always moaning about being at home,' he sighed.

'Yeah, great night out watching your husband flirt with every female around.'

'Leave it, Maddy. It's only a bit of fun. You've got to get out more and make an effort to talk to people. You'd like them.'

'I've seen their looks, Christophe, especially the brunette giggling like a schoolgirl.'

'Come on, Madeline! You know her, she used to teach the kids on the slopes near the village. She's a work colleague, for God's sake!'

'I don't believe you. Why don't you just leave me and get on with your life.'

'Two things, Maddy. I love you and I need to work to earn money for both of us…and part of that is networking with the staff.'

'So it's my fault now because I can't earn a living.'

'I give up…you just don't listen, do you? I want to be with you.'

Madeline's sulking continued on the journey home, interspersed with occasional harsh barbs directed towards Christophe – who had decided long ago it was sometimes best to keep quiet.

Occasionally, Madeline felt Christophe's charm work on her in bed, when he kissed and reassured her she was the only one for him. 'Those bunnies are just a bit of fluff…nothing to worry about, sweetheart.' Perhaps things would improve after all, she told herself.

Madeline, satisfied for the moment, would snuggle in, and succumb to sleep, only to be woken early by Christophe's car revving. He'd pull out at dawn to head up the mountain for another long day on the slopes – and in the bars.

Spring brought some relief during warmer months when the snow and ice dissolved from their property's access road. Madeline was once again able to drive to visit friends and maintain some independence – getting out and about served to temporarily lift her spirits.

However, every year, when the season changed and winter lay its fog and drizzle once more over the snow gums, Madeline's mind curled into itself. Confined again, she busied herself with things to fill in the day. Trapped was what she called it – in her log cabin. She spent hours browsing the Internet, quilting, cooking, reading and lounging about watching midday movies. Usually, this was followed by an afternoon nap, until she returned to the kitchen to prepare dinner and stoke the fireplace. The evenings were becoming cooler and Madeline incessantly asked Christophe to ensure there was enough firewood. His responses gradually turned from 'Of course, my darling,' to 'Stop nagging me.'

A pattern set over them like a blanket of snow when each laid out different itineraries for their day. Christophe was always in the company of others, while Madeline was more often alone. She did, however, try each evening to be pleasant when serving up tasty creations. She knew Christophe liked her cooking because he wolfed every mouthful and wiped his lips in appreciation. 'Great dish, Maddy, must have taken a while to get the flavours so perfect.'

A tiny measure of joy washed over Maddy before she replied, 'Got to spend my day doing something.' She watched him flinch, knowing full well any reference to the skiing accident, however slight, still grated.

At first, Christophe would apologise about the accident. However, nowadays he tended to cast his eyes downward and leave the table without further conversation.

Madeleine knew it was a low blow…but somehow, she couldn't stop her fly-away remarks. Resentment towards her husband increased daily – and more so when she saw pictures in the local paper of him flanked either side by snow-tanned athletic girls. Compelled to steer the conversation back on track, she'd sometimes laugh it off and present a sweet soufflé or hot sticky date pudding with lashings of cream.

When Christophe's growing appetite for good food was satiated, Madeline would further endeavour to make amends in bed some nights through tender loving – something he couldn't resist.

Nevertheless, in the end, Madeline's bitterness tipped into every aspect of their lives. While Christophe never outwardly displayed anger towards her, he managed the situation in the only way he knew – by distancing himself. Emotionally and physically. The art of saying nothing left Madeline feeling punished for her narky comments.

Ultimately, it was his indifference, unshakable by any means or caress, which marked the end. He didn't even offer a snarl over the barbs she threw, or sneer at her attempts to quell her rants.

One morning, Madeline stumbled down the staircase dropping a full basket of quilting fabrics and threads.

Christophe lent a hand to pull her up. 'Are you okay?' he asked, unwinding her fingers which were gripping his arm.

Madeline sniffed and dabbed a tear. 'Um…I think so.'

Christophe didn't turn to face her when he skittered through the front door. It was a defining, forever moment, when she felt the full force of his apathy towards her, which somehow suppressed any attempts she felt to rekindle their marriage wane.

At times, Madeline wondered if her perception was misconstrued – perhaps she just couldn't face the truth when it finally came down to this. The gap seemed too wide to bridge and any light in their relationship had extinguished. Regaining some control of her situation, she retrieved her car keys from Christophe's van while he slept. Madeline weighed up her options, where she might go and what she could do, but nothing amounted to a tangible plan. The winter days and nights were long, and she conjured up imaginary scenarios of Christophe with other women. During these times, Madeline felt her entire body rack with jealousy and rage, which left her exhausted. She slumped into sleep only to wake in the morning with red marks on her arms from clawing herself in the night. Lamenting her lost life, she whispered, 'I'll never forgive you, Christophe. It's all your doing.'

One night ,Madeline lay awake staring out the window at the night sky. A slip of a crescent moon was obscured by floating clouds. It was damp and dark when she waited for Christophe's return. Her ears picked up on the distinctive giggle of a girl she'd seen hanging off her husband one night at the pub. Obviously, Christophe once again had overindulged with too much grog and needed a lift home. When she noticed the car had pulled away and her husband had been dropped off at the top of their access road, Madeline listened carefully to his footsteps crunch on the long gravel driveway, leading to their cabin. Panic set into Madeline when a driving force of revenge surfaced. She pushed herself up and sat on the edge of the bed, threw her tracksuit on, and headed to the garage. She revved the car engine with her hand hard on the modified accelerator and sped up the drive.

Startled, like a roo caught in the car headlights, Christophe watched, frozen like a statue, when the vehicle skidded straight for him.

Thud…the car groaned to a halt.

First

Leah and James cruised on his thirty-five-foot yacht, searching for a place to moor overnight. Near the end of the day, they found a somewhat protected area at the western edge of the beach. James released the sheets to let the sails flap, then tossed the anchor and chain over the bow. The white sand shone like a beacon along the entire Esperance coast. Once the boat was secured, they let down the rear transom and tested the water. Translucent waves lapped at their toes and though a tad cool, even in the summer months, the sea tantalised. On such a radiant day with hardly a breath of wind, the afternoon beckoned a final swim. They were ready to take advantage of the clear conditions for a snorkel and a surf in case the weather blew up later – which was always a possibility when the wind gusted north from the Southern Ocean. Leah looked back on their day together and shook her head, recalling how strange it was, that things could change in a split-second, which was all it took.

It was no surprise to Leah how quickly James had become enamoured with the Australian coast and climate, after living most of his life in England. He'd come from a wealthy family back home, but also made good money for himself down south in the Antipodes, his favoured name for the continent. Leah was somewhat in awe of his ability to achieve anything he set his mind to, in a relatively short space of time. At the moment, James was doing very well in his photography business and she was also quietly proud of him, even though she didn't praise him directly, because James tended to be full of himself anyway. He didn't need someone else adding to his vanity and pompous ways. Notwithstanding, Leah felt herself falling in love with him. She secretly harboured the idea that she and James might end up together – but that was a way off at this stage of their courtship.

Leah also liked the way James cared for her – a bit old-fashioned – yet she lapped it up. She also felt flattered when he constantly photographed her. James was always fiddling with his camera lenses, aiming for the perfect shot. Leah was in most photos, except for his seascapes, which had won him much acclaim.

Once everything was in order and the boat secured, James asked, 'What do you reckon, Leah? One last swim before we find a lee shore for the night?'

'Sure, why not,' Leah replied, before she gathered her flippers, snorkel and mask, and grabbed her blue and white striped bikini from below. She knew once she was in the ocean, James would be alongside underwater taking her photo. Leah cherished the attention he gave her when she was posing and twirling like a model.

Swimming and snorkelling, the pair circled and swayed against each other. When James had completed snapping all the photos he required, he surfaced and climbed up the transom ladder onto the boat to check his shots. Leah enjoyed a bit more freedom in the water before she boarded, relishing the last moments before setting sail to somewhere more sheltered for their overnight anchorage.

Once the anchor was retrieved and the sails hoisted, they set off. The weather was balmy and the sea a little choppy, yet the swell was building and black clouds gathered at the horizon. Leah took control of trimming the sails, while James steered. They settled into an easy rhythm, when out of nowhere the unpredictable Southern Ocean climate blew up a squall. The yacht was knocked on its side and rounded up, just as the mainsail jibed. Crack. In a split second, Leah glimpsed a flash before the boom threw her sideways onto the deck. Precariously close to being swept overboard, Leah held tight onto a stanchion. As the yacht righted itself, she rubbed her head. In a foggy daze, she felt a trickle of blood seep into the palm of her hand.

When the boat sails flapped back onto a different tack, James steadied their course and held a hand out to grab Leah. 'You okay?' he called.

'Yes, I think so,' Leah said, positioning herself once more to trim the headsail. She wanted to say more yet wasn't sure what – something untoward niggled inside her. She clamped her mouth shut to prevent words escaping. Best wait until we're in a safe harbour, she warned herself.

Late in the afternoon when the boat was safely moored for the night, Leah ventured below to check out any items which may have come loose when the jibe occurred. She then came topside with their usual bottle of wine, along with peanuts and olives to snack on before she went below again to the galley to prepare dinner. She was glad James liked her cooking. However, if truth be known, she was getting a bit jack of being chief cook and bottle washer, as her mum would say.

James remained on deck fiddling with camera lenses, making sure the glass in them was secure.

Leah handed him a glass of chilled Riesling. 'How's your camera?

'Okay, thanks. Nearly lost it. Luckily, I grabbed the strap.'

Leah paused, then remembered what she meant to say earlier. 'First!'

'Huh?' James looked quizzically at her, while he continued wiping saltwater spots off the tiny convex camera lenses with a soft cloth.

'I meant, luckily you grabbed the strap…FIRST! Before you held out your hand for me.'

James tilted his head and opened his mouth to speak but not a word escaped. Silence. Leah heard James's silence, loud and clear.

Swamping down two Panadol with wine, Leah dabbed her congealing cut, then rubbed a little Hirodoid to ease the bruised egg mounting on her forehead. Anything further she wanted to say stuck in her throat. It saddened her when she understood James didn't quite get the point of her dilemma. What he'd done in a crisis could not be undone. She fussed about clearing glasses and snack bowls.

'Can I help?' James offered, still somewhat puzzled.

'No thanks,' she whispered and went below alone.

Leah studied her bruised face in the mirror and attempted to re-evaluate her relationship with James. Did James really appreciate the fullness of her as a partner, or was she to remain a two-dimensional image through his camera lens?

Carpe Noctem

Arabella Heatherington was surprised when her boyfriend of about six months, William Wylde, proposed. Her heart went aflutter. Cherishing his exact words, she folded them away in her mind, like a secret note to be kept forever.

She had recently turned twenty-five and her whole life loomed ahead. University days ended in 1980 and she was ready to travel the world, before coming back to a promising career in a local legal firm in the thriving coastal township of Coffs Harbour.

However, things swiftly changed when Bella recalled the words of Will's announcement after dinner one evening. He finger-curled a titian lock of hair from her forehead. 'Bella, you are perfect for me. I'm asking you to marry me.'

The word perfect sounded so special, so all encompassing – just right. Bella wasn't aware Will felt so strongly about her, yet at the same time charmed by this man who was so openly besotted with her. She certainly wasn't expecting his proposal so soon, even though, when she grew to know him better, she grasped how he liked to strategise and steer things along. A good sign, Bella considered. At least we'll get somewhere in life. Maybe even afford our own home one day, not like some of those no-hopers my girlfriends have hitched up with. She also didn't want to let Will go, knowing a few others had him in their sights. I suppose travel can wait, she convinced herself. After all, it's not everyday someone comes along like Will Wylde and proposes. How lucky am I, she convinced herself.

A memory flash emerged unbidden from deep within. Bella shuddered when she recollected her mother's tragic marriage. Oftentimes, Bella's childhood days were tainted with episodes of yelling, swearing and violence during years of abuse from her father – now gone, thank God.

'Well, Belle baby, what's your answer?' Will beamed as he fiddled in his jacket pocket for a tiny green box.

Jolted from her reverie, Bella reacted to Will's question. 'Sorry…I was just thinking about marriage.'

'And?'

'Of course, I'll marry you.' Bella hugged him close while he fished out the box and held her at arm's length.

Opening the lid, Will placed the perfectly fitted ring on her left-hand third finger.

Bella smiled inwardly at Will's self-assurance at having the ring made ahead of time – and being so sure of her answer – and his assumption she would like the ring. The glittery emerald sat surrounded by tiny specks of diamond in a yellow gold setting. Possibly not her choice, because she had always imagined a solitaire set in rose gold to match a couple of handed-down pieces of antique jewellery she owned.

Notwithstanding a tinge of disappointment, Bella was not about to complain. She stared adoringly at the ring. 'It's beautiful and it fits so well!'

'I checked the size from your other ones.' Will grinned at his own ingenuity.

The next day, Bella decided to visit her mother to relay the good news – made all the better by the opportunity to finally have a shorter name. Henceforth, she'd write on all documents, Bella Wylde, or wild Belle, if the situation called for it.

Arriving early morning, Bella knocked once at her mother's unlocked door. She proceeded inside when she heard her mum call.

'Just finishing pegging out the washing. Put the kettle on. Won't be long.'

Bella flicked the button on the already filled kettle and waited alongside the mantelpiece of cluttered family photos. Her gaze fixated on a picture of her parents' wedding day. Bella's mum looked gorgeous in a long ivory silk-satin gown with a train about two metres long. She could almost smell the bouquet scent of stephanotis, a flower which had remained a favourite of her mum's. Her father looked handsome in a plain dark suit and tie. Both were smiling at each other. Looking genuinely joyful, Bella thought. They seemed like a perfect match. Whatever went wrong, she pondered. She'd ask her mum about it. Maybe not now, though.

When her mum returned from outside, the kettle whistled and her mother promptly dunked a couple of tea bags into their mugs. A far cry from the old days, Bella noted, when we had to wait for the Lan Choo tea leaves to settle in the pot.

Bella made an overt flourish with her left hand as she extracted a ginger nut biscuit from the jar. The look of pleasure on her daughter's face didn't go unnoticed by her mother, nor the sparkle of the new ring.

'Okay…tell me all about it,' her mum probed.

Bella, eager to blurt out the whole scenario in a single phrase, held back and started at the beginning. She told her mum how romantic the past months had been, how attentive and thoughtful Will was, all of which culminated in those few words, 'perfect…marry me.'

Once the initial excitement had subsided and a sketchy outline of the wedding plan hatched, Bella summoned the courage to ask to her mum about something which was bothering her.

'Mum, I know your life with Dad was tough most of the time, and I can't help wondering if the same could happen to me.'

Bella's mum instinctively felt a flush of anxiety creep along the nape of her neck. She faced her daughter and reassured her. 'It won't, sweetie. We live in different times. In my day, we just got married, had kids and often no career. I'm sure you won't let it happen to you.'

Bella stiffened as if she'd woken from a bad dream when she further related her worries to her mother. 'I sometimes wake from nightmares where I'm wanting to save myself from some sort of scary monster or someone about to harm me.' She paused before adding. 'I think I know what the dreams are about. In the past, I let someone else step in and take the blows, and that was you, Mum. As a child, I missed out on being hit because I tried to save my own skin first. I mutely stood by while you were being hurt.' She saw her mother wince and avoid looking directly at her. Bella was determined not to let the moment pass, now she finally had the opportunity to reveal what had been bothering her for years.

Bella continued, 'Your muffled wails from the locked bedroom became commonplace after a while. I was only a child, yet I knew you were taking the beatings behind the locked door. I knew when I called out and you answered in your tiny, strained voice, "I'm all right, just go outside to play," you were protecting all of us. We kids were supposed to play outside until dark, but sometimes it was raining or cold, so we crept inside to play.' Bella dabbed an escaping tear. 'That's when we heard your cries from behind the door.'

Her mother spoke. 'Your father's abuse was often due to his unfounded jealously and suspicions, usually after a session at the pub. Those times were grim. I knew it would eventually blow over, but I couldn't let anything happen to you kids.'

'Mum, even though you told us you were all right, from a young age we knew it wasn't true. We were silenced. I suppose it was the only way to keep the peace until the next time.'

Bella watched her mother visibly switch into a calmer mode, as if whatever happened in the past had somehow flowed away on a lunar tide.

Her mother then urged her, 'You should let go of those old fears. It was so long ago,' she sighed. 'You have to understand there was no use in all of you kids getting hurt if I could keep him away from you. It's what a mother does. Protects her children.'

Bella felt as if her mother had silenced her again, so she pressed on. 'Tell me this, Mum, how did it start? In your wedding photo, you look so happy. I just don't get it!'

'It crept up on me bit by bit. Insidious,' her mother said. 'One day things are fine and, before you know it, they've turned for the worse.

Too late to change things. By then, you're in too far – kids, no money and nowhere to go to in those days. So I stuck it out and hoped things might change.'

Bella hugged her mum and prepared her things ready to leave, knowing she'd be back in a couple of days to delve into full-on wedding mode with her mum, who'd always been there to help sort things out.

Bella's mum called her back from the door. 'Don't forget your honeymoon. Any thoughts yet?'

'No. Every time I bring it up, Will seems to deflect onto other more important things, like business opportunities or looking for a house we can afford – he says there'll be plenty of time later to travel.'

'Belle, you're only young and free once, so make the most of a small trip before you're tied down. Wish I had.'

A sense of disquiet lingered on Bella's way home. She understood, even though her mother took the rap to save her children from their father's rages, the real damage of knowing what had taken place behind the closed door still festered inside. It was her burden now and there was no way she was going to broach the subject with her mum again. After all, her mum was a survivor and optimistic in her outlook on life, doing the things which she couldn't do while her husband was alive. Her mother was independent and fun-loving now she had the time to travel and become more involved with her grandkids.

Nevertheless, Bella knew her own gut still churned when she thought about her early years. The guilt she felt because she hadn't intervened enough, hence leaving her mum to suffer, still nagged inside. As Bella grew older, she had tried. However, her attempts seemed pitifully weak. By then, the pattern was set, and her father was too powerful, strong and threatening for her siblings and herself to speak up. I should have stopped it, but I didn't, she scolded herself.

Bella perpetually questioned her behaviour, or lack of it. I wonder where that leaves me? Am I a coward? Bella was left with the disturbing knowledge she had formed and embedded in herself a state of self-survival, whereby she could so willingly put herself first while someone else suffered. It was this survival instinct which would pull her through anything – if she ever needed to harness her inner strength to sustain her relationship. Hmm…maybe Mum's right and I should press harder to plan a honeymoon with Will. Feeling a twinge of guilt at her own selfishness, Bella reassured herself how much Will loved her. She was certain he would never act like her dad. There was no way she would allow herself to stay in a marriage like her mother had.

The wedding planning progressed, and the day beckoned. Bella felt increasingly unsettled and restless, especially late one evening after Will had dropped her back to her flat – after a short spat about honeymoons venues. She'd eventually given in to his idea to put the honeymoon off until they were settled in their own place. Pre-wedding jitters, she told herself.

Sometimes, Bella would fall asleep only to find herself awake a couple of hours later, wrapped in damp sheets like a strangler vine. These times evoked memories of her mother being awake most nights, when Bella was in her late teens and out partying. Her mum would always call out nightie-night when her daughter arrived home in the wee small hours of morning. It was one of the many ways her mum loved and protected her children. Bella decided to ask her mother how she coped with those sleepless nights, so made a point of ringing her the following morning.

'Simple,' her mother recalled. 'I found my serenity in the night when your dad was snoring and the household asleep. I'd slip outside into the still cool air and stargaze. *Carpe noctem.*'

A full year had passed since their wedding day before Bella and Will slipped away to celebrate a belated honeymoon, a weekend at a Byron Bay beach resort. It was far from the overseas travel Bella had imagined for herself, but given the time constraints with Will's business commitments, she was grateful to escape their busy home and work lives at all. The New South Wales north coast was a doable car trip from where they lived, and certainly a beautiful place to relax and rejuvenate.

After their first deckchair cocktail, the usual admonishments began, when Bella sucked her tummy in and attempted to squeeze into her cossie.

'Hey, Belle, I think you need to lose a few kilos, or I'll be buying you a new swimsuit again.' Will chuckled as if it were a joke, then playfully nabbed the sticky cherry-laden toothpick from her glass and downed the fruit in one swoop.

'Don't worry, I intend to by Christmas.'

'You said that last Christmas.'

'Sorry, I'll really try this time,' Bella groaned, knowing how much she relished her food and all the fancy restaurants they frequented.

'Still, I'm a lucky man to have you,' Will smiled, heaved a sigh, and added, 'You're as close to perfect anyone could wish for. Now let's have a swim.' Will dived straight into the deep end of the pool and started doing laps.

Bella felt stung. It was only a year ago she was considered perfect in his eyes and now she only ranked close to perfect. She didn't reply, though tucked the comment away in her heart with all the other little stings of late. She mused over a recent dinner party conversation where Will suggested she change her hairstyle to match a new style he liked on her closest girlfriend. Another time, he complained about everything she had cooked for a whole week, including his favourite dishes, which she'd fussed over. There were constant jibes about her flowy clothes and dress style in general, even though she felt she had kept up with latest trends. Will had seemed so charming and devoted to her when they were first married. However, now it seemed she couldn't do anything right.

Bella pushed herself up from the deckchair and ambled to the edge of the pool. Tentatively, she dipped her toe in the chilly water, too cold for her liking. She was about to turn around and retreat, when in an instant Will torpedoed out from an underwater glide and splashed her with a wave of water. It almost sent her screeching back to the warmth of her towel. Too late, Bella thought knowing she was already soaked.

Tears welled in her eyes. She was about to howl. She refused to give Will the satisfaction of seeing her cry. The only way to avoid him was to jump straight into the pool. Downward, Bella sunk into the quiet of underwater. Mum, I think I get it now.

Mica Beach

There's a place up north called Mica Beach. It's nestled in tropical aquamarine waters a few kilometres west of Fannie Bay in Darwin. Mica, flaky thin and sparkling, washes to and fro in ripples onto the sand, as if someone has flung buckets full of silver confetti into the sea. Glistening under sunshine, the beach dulls in late afternoon when the sun dips behind the hill providing shade, a relief from unrelenting heat. It was a place Jules would never forget.

Jules worked a mixture of short shifts at the sailing club, in the kitchen or the bar. She soon became acquainted with the diaspora who flocked to Darwin. There were long-time locals who had survived cyclones and droughts, along with many transients, those folk who seemed to be running from something, or too something, eventually drifting in and out doing odd jobs up and down the track, the home-grown name for the Stuart Highway, which ran from the city to Alice Springs.

Jules's shift was nearly ended when she mopped the bar slops for the umpteenth time that day. She wiped her forehead, took off her apron, undid her ponytail and flicked her chestnut hair free. The sailor, the one known as skipper Dan – to distinguish him from the other Dan blow-ins – was a local. He left the bar as it closed, taking with him with a couple of beers. Beckoning Jules to join him, he sat at a table on the grass under the shadow of a palm tree.

'Finished at last,' Jules said. 'It's this damned humidity. I can't cope with it.'

'Don't worry, you get used to the build-up after a few years.'

'Don't think I'll hang around that long.'

'Wait till the wet breaks in a couple of months. It'll cool down then.'

Dan offered her a glass and Jules gulped it half down before she took a breath.

'You've developed a taste for the local beer.' Dan smiled.

'Guess so. It's cold.' Jules gazed over the bay watching the skies turn pink then red before the fireball sun slipped away. 'Still can't get used to facing the water at sunset.'

'That's just the position we face from here. Over at Mica Beach, it's the opposite.'

'Yeah, someone told me about that beach.'

'I take my boat over there a bit. Maybe we can set sail one day and see the sparkles?'

Jules observed Dan, so sure of himself with his rugged sun-baked features, bleached hair and cheeky grin. Did she detect a twinkle in his steel-blue eyes? Jules had only known Dan a couple of weeks when he'd brought his yacht back into Darwin waters, in preparation for putting it up on the hard stand before the wet broke. She had only been in Darwin for six months, travelling around the territory after finishing uni on the east coast in NSW. Bars and waitressing had funded some touring and her rent, but not a lot of extras. A sailing trip to Mica Beach sounded exciting.

'Sure, love to.'

'Gotta watch the big tides up here. They can be up to forty feet. It runs in and out fast on the turn.'

'I don't understand.'

'It means we leave at half-tide, spend some time on the beach while the water's high and head back before it runs out – so we don't get caught on a sandbank.'

'Sounds complicated.'

'Being stranded isn't the best way to end a good day, believe me.'

'Okay, when can we go?'

Dan looked outward at the skies, the breeze line on the water, the current and the sea level. He checked his watch. 'Perhaps around eleven tomorrow. I'll bring some cold beers on ice, maybe you could rustle up some sandwiches.'

'Sure. I need to be at work by five, though. Boss wants me to back-up for happy hour in the bar.'

'All right, we can manage that.'

Jules finished her beer, wondering where exactly Mica Beach sat amongst the headlands. She stood to go. 'See you then.'

The next day was cloudy, steamy and hot. Loading the esky filled with ice and beer, Dan set about preparing the boat. Jules wore her magenta bikini underneath a loose cotton shirt and navy shorts. She threw in her work gear for later, plus a sunhat and sunscreen.

They set off to the yacht in the small rowboat, which they attached with a tow rope to the stern. It would be needed for getting in and out of the shore at Mica Beach.

Jules was mesmerised when she splashed about the shallows watching the colours of mica crystals breaking into pearly lustres of grey, sage green and sometimes purple. Playing with larger chunks, she separated the sheets of mica with her fingernails to reveal translucent and opaque shades.

The day consisted of affable chatting while Dan expertly flicked bottle tops off with the opener on his Swiss army knife. After the sandwiches were eaten, they rested on their towels and sun-baked.

Dan was the first to break the dreamy state Jules had lulled into. He offered to spread sunscreen on her back and, in doing so, bent down and kissed her neck. She turned, intending to say something off-putting, when his lips pressed hard on her mouth with a prolonged kiss.

Jules broke away. 'Hey, sorry, Dan, but I just see you as a friend.'

Dan seemed a bit miffed. However, he backed off and settled down to sunbake and talk about the thrills of wild storms in the wet season and the big Christmas tides.

Jules segued into the mention of tides. 'Shouldn't we be getting back soon before the run-out tide?'

'One more kiss and we'll get going.' Dan flashed a cheeky smile. 'You wouldn't want to get stranded on a sandbank.'

Jules, recognising his hidden agenda, leant over and pecked him on the cheek. 'There you are. Now let's go.'

'I meant a proper kiss.' Dan positioned his body on top of Jules and kissed her voraciously.

She gasped for breath when he grabbed both her hands above her head and held tight. Jules squirmed to free herself, except she was pinned to the ground. Dan yanked off her bikini bottom and then wedged one knee to open her legs, before thrusting himself inside her.

Jules yelled. However, there was no one on the deserted beach. Defeated, she turned her head away and scrunched her eyes shut. She felt like vomiting when she was overcome by his smell, his sweat, his strength…his shudder.

And then. It was over.

Dan rolled off and stood, pulling up his shorts.

Brittle, like a snapped twig, Jules's voice cracked. 'I want…to go back… NOW.'

'Soon. I need to pee first.' Dan headed to the bushes.

Jules watched from a distance as he fiddled near a tree. She then entered the sea and scrubbed her skin with handfuls of mica-laden sand grit. Time to go. We're going now, she reassured herself when Dan returned and launched the rowboat. The tide was still quite high when they loaded their gear. Jules prayed they wouldn't end up on a sandbank.

Setting sail toward the western shore, Dan seemed a tad wary of Jules's abrupt manner. 'Something bothering you, Jules?'

'You know what you did.'

'I thought you wanted me. You seemed to like it at first.'

'I didn't. You forced yourself on me.'

'But I…'

'Stop! I don't want to hear your excuses.'

The remainder of the journey was silent. Upon their arrival and once securely anchored in water deep enough for the yacht's keel, they climbed into the rowboat and headed for shore. Jules couldn't get out of the boat quick enough. She almost dropped her work gear into the water when she jumped off in the shallows. Retrieving her bag, she rushed toward the sailing club change-room and pulled herself together. Jules wanted to scream, she wanted to sob, yet she would do neither. She was going to finish her shift and get far away from this place.

Once ensconced with a couple of workmates, Jules passed off their enquiries about her sailing trip with a few pleasantries and moved on to serving customers. She had little to say to them yet managed to get the beers out fast. Fetching frosted schooner glasses, she pulled the draught lever and filled beer to the top of the rim where it overflowed. Everyone liked to see a good head on their beer and Jules was tipped for her efforts.

Old Charlie, a regular, called from the end of the bar. 'G'day, Jules. Schooner down here thanks.'

Jules obliged and plonked his beer within his reach, then attempted to turn to the next customer.

'You're a bit quiet today. What's up? Cat got your tongue?' Charlie called out.

Jules made light of his comments. 'No, Charlie, just having a busy shift.'

'I wanted to ask you how your sailing venture went over at Mica.'

'Fine, just fine.' Jules turned her face.

'Did Dan show you his tree?'

'Huh?'

Charlie stifled a belch after gulping his beer. He wiped the froth from his grey whiskers and looked her in the eye. 'The one where he carves all his notches.'

Jules lowered her eyes and felt her neck burn. Her cheeks flashed crimson when she sensed what Charlie was alluding to. She was also aware of the extent the locals protected their mates.

Dan noticed Charlie talking with Jules, so swaggered toward the end of the bar. She saw him approach and promptly wiped down the bar and untied her apron, ready to bolt.

Dan stepped into her path. 'You okay?'

'Of course not. What do you think?'

'Can we talk, have a drink outside?'

'No. I'm leaving now.' Jules continued walking and a shiver ran through her entire being. Why, she thought, do I feel so cold in this relentless heat?

Contemplating what to do, Jules knew there would be ramifications, whatever line she pursued. One thing was certain, though – what happened on Mica Beach would be with her forever, dividing her life trajectory into before and after.

Jules yearned to go somewhere, anywhere. She needed to flee this place, to be alone, to think. At least for now.

About the Author

Liz Newton was born in Australia and currently lives in Sydney with her husband and dog. She has three adult children and seven grandchildren.

Extensive travelling, including road trips across continents, sailing adventures and family holidays, has provided inspiration for creative writing and photography.

Liz has worked in health services, in particular mental health, including drug and alcohol, in a variety of roles, as well as teaching and tutoring at universities and involvement in health research and ethics.

Her academic background is in anthropology and comparative sociology. Research has included exploring issues of indigenous suicide, vocational training opportunities for people with mental health issues, and a PhD doctoral thesis on the ethnography of deinstitutionalisation for people with mental illness, resulting in many peer-reviewed publications.

More recently, Liz has enjoyed the freedom and creativity of fiction writing, and has published two novels, *Faraway on an Island* and *Jagged Edge of Joy*, as well as *Meandering*, a selection of short stories, some of which have been awarded in competitions. More recently her memoir *The Firing Line* was shortlisted in the Society of Women Writers 2021 awards.